Judith and Spider

For Vanessa, who wanted to know more about Judith

Judith and Spider

Mike Scott

First published 1992 by
WOLFHOUND PRESS
68 Mountjoy Square,
Dublin 1

Wolfhound Press receives financial assistance from The Arts Council / An Chomhairle Ealaíon, Dublin, Ireland.

This book is fiction. All characters, incidents and names have no connection with any persons, living or dead. Any apparent resemblance is purely coincidental.

British Library Cataloguing in Publication Data
Scott, Michael
    Judith and Spider
    I. Title
    823.914 [J]

    ISBN 0-86327-347-5

Cover design and illustration: Peter Haigh
Typesetting: Wolfhound Press
Printed by the Guernsey Press Co Ltd, Guernsey, Channel Isles

Saturday 16th January

1

— A face in the crowd.
— Briefly glimpsed.
— Gone.

Judith Meredith turned quickly, but the unseasonably warm day and the January Sales had combined to fill Henry Street with a sea of bodies and by the time she had turned, the face was lost.

Standing on her toes, she searched the crowd, her head turning from side to side. It was hopeless; her chances of spotting anyone .... There! She was turning back to Roches Stores window when she spotted the face again on the opposite side of the street, beside Arnotts. She stared hard at the narrow, deeply-tanned face, suddenly unsure, though she had been certain a few seconds before. Even when the tall young man turned and she noticed that the jet-black hair was tied back into a neat ponytail, she still wasn't finally convinced. 'Spider?' she wondered. Even as she spoke his name the young man half-turned and glanced over his shoulder.

It *was* Spider!

Judith felt her heart lurch and a sudden lump filled her throat. Her stomach began somersaulting. Swallowing hard, she desperately resisted the urge to throw up.

She had met Spider six months earlier and had one of the most exciting and exhilarating weeks of her life with him. She had learned more in those five days with the young traveller than she had learned in all of her fifteen years. But the adventure had ended in pain and disaster for both of them. They had driven through a garda road-block only to encounter a second one a few miles down the road. And these guards were armed. The van Spider had been driving had overturned when the guards had fired on it, and both Judith and Spider had barely escaped with their lives. Although under constant supervision in the hospital, Spider managed to escape. Judith never expected to see him again, although she treasured the three-word note he had sent her in hospital: *I love you*.

That had been six months ago. And now here he was: standing less than a hundred yards away.

Judith reached across and squeezed her sister-in-law's shoulder. 'I'll see you back at the car in a couple of hours.'

'Where are you going?' Peggy asked quickly. The small stout woman bobbed up on her toes, looking around nervously.

'I'm going to buy a few tapes,' Judith lied. She was watching Spider's reflection in the glass window behind Peggy, knowing that if she turned around, the woman would know that something was wrong.

'Well ... all right,' Peggy conceded. She glanced at her watch.' It's one now; be sure to be back at the car by three.'

'I'll be there,' Judith promised.

'And be careful,' Peggy added.

'I'll be sixteen next birthday,' Judith said indignantly, 'I can look after myself.' She turned away from Peggy and allowed the crowd to carry her along, knowing that the smaller woman would quickly lose sight of her. Judith concentrated on getting across the street to where she'd last seen Spider, but was dismayed to discover that he'd gone. When she reached Arnott's window, she stood on her toes, staring down the street.

Where was he? Where had he gone?

Judith felt her eyes fill with tears. It had been Spider! She was convinced of it. And it wasn't fair that he should have been so close and was now gone. It just wasn't fair! Moving down the street, she kept close to the shop windows, her head turning from side to side, scanning the crowd.

She spotted him coming out of HMV.

Judith pushed her way almost roughly through the crowd. Some of the Saturday morning shoppers turned to look at the blond, well-dressed young woman, and muttered about her rudeness. But Judith didn't care; she didn't even hear them.

Spider seemed to be in a hurry. His shoulders were hunched, hands dug deep into the pockets of his scuffed leather jacket. He stopped at the entrance to the GPO Arcade, and raised his head to look up in the direction of O'Connell Street. Judith was just about to call out his name when he suddenly disappeared into the arcade. She ran after him, slipping and almost falling on the smooth floor of the refurbished and renovated shopping arcade. She spotted Spider running out the far end.

She was also in time to see that he was being chased by a tall, wild-haired youth. They both turned to the right and vanished from her sight.

Judith spun round, desperately looking for a garda. Spider was in trouble, she was sure of it. And then she stopped. The police were the last people Spider would want involved. Only she could help him now. Taking a deep breath, she raced down the length of the arcade, her heels clicking on the ground. She skidded to a halt at the jeans shop and turned to the right. But it seemed to be a dead end. To her left was Penneys and the GPO, but she was sure she'd seen Spider turn this way. Maybe he'd run into one of the buildings in the narrow cul-de-sac, but which one? And why had he been running?

It took Judith a moment to realise that there was a narrow alleyway beyond a small black pillar to her left. Although born and raised in Dublin, she had spent very little time in the city itself, and of course, never on her own. Usually when she was taken to Dublin she would be going somewhere — shopping, the theatre, an exhibition, a gallery — and so her knowledge of the main streets was pretty sketchy, and she was completely unfamiliar with the backstreets.

A shout, a scream of curses, brought her running to the mouth of the alley. She stopped and peered in. A stout balding man, much older than Spider, had caught him around the chest, pinning his arms to his side, while the tall red-haired youth Judith had spotted earlier, was swinging at Spider with his fists. Spider was holding him back by lashing out with his feet.

'Spider!' Judith screamed.

For a single moment, everyone froze. The tall youth turned to look behind him, and in that instant the point of Spider's boot caught him in the kneecap. Howling, the youth crashed to the ground, cradling his knee in both hands. Spider then drove his heel back into the shin of the man holding him. With a shout of pain, he released Spider and staggered back into the wall. Spider hopped over the youth on the ground, grabbed Judith's hand and dragged her from the alleyway. 'Let's go,' he panted.

There were a thousand questions she wanted to ask him, but as they dodged through the crowds on O'Connell Street, across the bridge, down Westmoreland Street and around by Trinity College, Judith found she hadn't got time to ask him anything. He set a pace that wasn't quite a run, but still left her breathless. He kept looking around nervously, and his hand, in hers, was sweating.

He slowed as they entered Grafton Street and then, deliberately and self-consciously, released Judith's hand. He searched through the pockets of his leather jacket and finally found a scrap of a paper handkerchief which he used to wipe his forehead.

Judith Meredith had rehearsed her meeting with Spider a hundred times. She knew exactly how it was going to go; she knew the expressions she would assume, the tone of voice she would use, how she would fix him with her eyes and demand to know why he hadn't contacted her over the previous six months. She had her speech ready and knew it by heart. But she forgot it all. Instead, she said, 'Are you always in trouble, Spider?'

'Always,' he said with a quick grin and for a moment he was exactly as she remembered him, but then the grin faded and the lines etched themselves on to his face, around his eyes and mouth. He looked ... ill, she decided.

'Are you OK? Are you hurt?'

'No, I'm not hurt. You saved me a beating though.'

'You don't look well,' Judith suggested quietly.

'I've had a cold.' He replied so quickly that she instinctively knew he was lying.

They walked in silence for a while. Grafton Street was slightly less crowded than Henry Street and filled with such a mixture of characters that no-one took any interest in the mis-matched young couple walking side-by-side up the street.

They were passing one of the fast-food restaurants when Judith caught Spider's sleeve and tugged him towards it. 'I'm dying for a cup of tea,' she said, forcing a smile to her lips. He nodded quickly, and as they stepped into the warmth, redolent of frying food, she distinctly heard his stomach rumble. 'Find us a seat,' she said. 'I'll get it.'

When she returned from the counter, carrying a tray laden with burgers, chips, hot apple-pie and tea, she discovered that Spider had found a corner seat half-hidden behind some plastic greenery, where he had his back to the wall and could watch the door. Spider nodded at the pile of food. 'I thought you said tea?' he said in his broad traveller accent.

'I haven't had lunch,' she said easily. 'I haven't eaten since breakfast and I'm hungry.'

A ghost of a smile twisted Spider's thin lips. 'No, you're not,' he said softly, 'you're just a bit peckish. I haven't eaten in two days. *I'm* hungry.' He said it casually, but she knew he wasn't lying, and suddenly she didn't feel quite so hungry any more.

Sitting back in the bright red plastic chair, Judith Meredith watched Spider pick his way through the chips, ignoring the burger. Looking at him critically, she realised that he was dirty. His hands were filthy, dirt encrusted under his nails, the spider tattoo on his right hand almost invisible beneath the grime. There was a layer of dirt on his skin, and his hair was shining with either grease or gel.

He caught her looking at him and raised his thick eyebrows in a silent question.

'I was wondering why you were only eating your chips?' she said quickly, not wanting him to know the real reason for her scrutiny.

'The chips get cold quicker,' he said, 'but the burger will stay hot in the box. So you eat the chips first, then the burger.' He smiled. 'That's one of the first rules you learn when you're living on the streets. You also learn not to bolt your food. Eat slowly, chew everything carefully, otherwise you'll get an awful case of the hiccups.'

Judith picked at her chips. 'I got your note in the hospital,' she said eventually.

Spider looked uncomfortable. Colour touched his cheeks. 'I'm glad you're OK,' he mumbled.

'I'm fine. What about you? I asked, but no-one would tell me. I discovered later that Daddy had instructed everyone that I was to be told nothing about you. All I learned was that you'd managed to slip out of the hospital.'

'I was lucky: a few cuts, a lot of bruises, nothing serious. But I knew if I hung around the police would have me. I just walked out of the place.' Finishing his chips, he opened the polystyrene box and lifted out the burger.

'I was hoping I'd hear from you,' Judith said, not looking at him.

Spider munched a big mouthful of burger and said nothing.

'I've never stopped thinking about you,' she continued.

Spider continued chewing, swallowed, drank some tea and swallowed again. 'Why?' he asked eventually.

Judith looked quickly at him. 'Do you have to ask?'

He nodded. 'I'm curious. You knew me for five days ....'

'You told me you loved me,' she hissed, lowering her voice.

Spider glanced away, not meeting her eyes. 'I did, didn't I?' he said very quietly.

'Did you mean it?'

'I meant it ... then.'

'And now?'

Spider put down his cup and looked at Judith. 'We knew one another for five days. That was a crazy time. And it was half a year ago. Time has passed. You're different. I'm different. Circumstances have changed.'

'What circumstances?' Judith demanded, blinking furiously, feeling tears pricking at the back of her eyes. For six months she had entertained a fantasy where she met Spider again and he would be delighted and the two of them could begin to make plans for a future together. And now her dream had come true ... except that it was turning into a nightmare.

Spider finished the last of his burger, and carefully unwrapped his apple-pie, picking away the cardboard wrapping, taking care not to burn his fingers.

'What circumstances?' Judith insisted.

Spider sighed. 'Six months ago, I drove a van at a guard Now, let's leave aside the fact that he was shooting at us at the time, but in their eyes, I endangered his life. The police have long memories; they never forgive, never forget. I have been hounded from county to county across Ireland; my description is in every station in every town and village across the country. My own people, the travellers, have been questioned again and again about me. If someone even resembling me is spotted in an area, all the travellers in that area are hassled. I've taken to avoiding them now.'

Judith shook her head, brushing strands of blonde hair off her face. 'There must be something more. Surely after six months the police wouldn't still be looking for you ....'

Spider held up a hand. 'Over the past six months a series of house burglaries and robberies have been committed by a young man who speaks with a traveller accent. The police think it's me. It's not, by the way, but that doesn't matter.' He looked away quickly, but she still saw the bitterness in his face. 'And then there's Kathleen and her brothers ... you remember Kathleen, don't you? She's the girl who thought you were taking me away from her, she's the one who wanted to fight you for me.'

'I remember her.' Judith said very quietly.

'Well, her two brothers, Mickser and Jed, are still looking for me, because we insulted their sister ... and wrecked their van. I spent five days with you, Judith Meredith, but while you were able to go back to your own people and your old way of life, I've been running every since, from the guards, from your people, even from my own. And, God help me, I'm tired, so tired.'

Judith was horrified by the note of despair in Spider's voice.

'Granny Hayes told me that you were bad news.' Spider's voice was very soft and Judith had to lean across the plastic table to hear him. 'She said that you were trouble.' He tried a laugh, which failed. 'But I always thought I could cope with trouble.' When he looked at Judith again, his dark eyes were bright, glistening. 'I never knew trouble until I met you, Judith Meredith. You have destroyed my life.'

Tears started to her own eyes and she reached across the table to lay her hand on his, her smooth, soft flesh and long painted nails bright against his darker, harder skin. 'I love you, Spider,' she said quickly.

'And I loved you ... until I realised it was a mistake.' Spider finished his tea quickly and crushed the cup in his fist. 'I don't love you now.'

2

Spider rose to his feet.

'You can't walk away from me now,' Judith said fiercely.

'What's to stop me?' Spider asked with a wry smile.

Judith was at a loss. 'Because ... because I'm asking you not to,' she said eventually. 'Please.'

Spider sank back into the seat. He looked at Judith's untouched food — she had only nibbled at a few chips — and said, 'Are you going to eat those?' When she shook her head, he pulled them towards him.

'They're cold,' Judith said, watching with distaste as he ate the greasy chips.

'I haven't eaten in two days; it might be another two before I eat again. When you're living on the street you learn never to waste any food.'

'I could get you some more,' Judith said quickly.

The dark-eyed traveller shook his head. 'No. Not just at the moment.'

Judith sat back and watched him finish off the cold food. Her thoughts were whirling. She was trying to reconcile the

Spider — she had known six months ago, calm, confident, controlled — with this rather unsure, nervous youth.

She went up to the counter and bought two more cups of tea. Spider accepted it with a grateful smile. He emptied four sachets of sugar into it, stirring the sticky mass with a white plastic spoon.

'You didn't always take so much sugar,' Judith remarked. 'You took three spoons.'

He seemed surprised that she remembered. 'It gives you energy,' he said simply.

'It's a false energy.'

'Maybe. But it's good enough for me.'

'Spider,' Judith said eventually, 'I want you to come home with me.'

He looked at her over the rim of the white cup, his eyes wide and disbelieving.

'It's all right,' she continued quickly. 'My parents are away. The house is empty. I'm staying with Peggy, my sister-in-law. She only lives down the road, but I'm studying for my exams and I've been up and down to my own house on a couple of occasions to get books and stuff.'

'And why would I want to come home to your house?' Spider asked quietly.

'You could rest, get some hot food, a bath. It would give you a little time to think. I don't think you can come to any conclusions when you're running around.'

Spider concentrated on the lukewarm tea. A warm bed, some hot water and food: it sounded like heaven. But his every instinct was warning him not to even think about it. The girl was trouble, nothing but trouble.

'I know I've caused you nothing but trouble,' she said quickly, echoing his thoughts. 'But maybe I can repay it a little. I even have some money which you'd be welcome to.'

'No,' Spider shook his head firmly. 'I may accept your hospitality, but I will not accept your charity.'

'I'm not offering you charity,' Judith said, almost angrily. 'Have you never had a friend, Spider?'

He looked at her for a moment, his face flat and expressionless. Then he dropped his gaze and stared into the murky tea. 'I've had friends.'

'You once told me you make a good friend, but a bad enemy.'

Spider nodded.

'We were friends once.' She was about to say more, but stopped. 'Let me help you — as a friend.'

Spider slowly finished the tea. Finally he looked up and said, 'Give me your address. I won't make any promises,' he added, 'but hot food, a hot bath and a soft bed are very tempting.'

When they left the restaurant, they walked down Grafton Street. Judith noticed how people instinctively moved out of Spider's way, but whether it was because of the way he looked — shabby, dishevelled and wild-eyed, his clothing dirty and stained — or because of the smell, she didn't know. She had been aware of the smell in the restaurant; there it had been masked by the smells of food, but in the open it was stronger, a pungent mixture of stale sweat, damp clothes and mildew.

A bearded, many-coated tramp spotted Spider and wove unsteadily across the street towards him. He stopped when he spotted Judith and squinted shortsightedly at the young man, suddenly unsure of his identity.

'Have you any money? Fifty pence or a pound, maybe?' Spider asked.

Judith dug into the pocket of her short leather jacket and produced a pound coin and some change. Spider plucked the pound from her outstretched palm. 'I'll pay it back,' he muttered, not looking at her. He went across to the tramp and pressed the coin into his grimy hand, and the two spoke quickly together for a few moments, while Judith stood up against Brown Thomas's window.

'A friend of yours?' Judith asked, when Spider eventually rejoined her.

'Sort of. On Christmas Day he bought me a cup of tea with his last pound coin.' A smile suddenly transformed his face and he was once again the Spider that Judith remembered. 'It felt good to be able to repay the money.'

'You were on the streets on Christmas Day?' Judith asked, unable to keep the note of horror from her voice.

Spider didn't answer her. He was watching two Gardai chatting together at the bottom of Grafton Street, and she could almost feel his tension. She knew that all they had to do was to look in his direction and he'd be gone.

Judith tugged his sleeve. 'Spider, listen to me. This is my address. In case ... in case we get separated or anything, this is where I will be for the rest of the night. I'll be waiting for you.'

Spider nodded, only half listening.

Judith told him the Killiney address, and made him repeat it until she was sure he had it right. Finally, she looked at her watch. She was shocked to discover nearly two hours had gone by. 'I've got to get back to the car. Peggy will probably call the police if I don't turn up in time.'

Spider nodded.

'Will you come tonight?' she asked anxiously.

'I'll think about it.'

'Promise,' she persisted.

'I said I'd think about it,' he snapped, and walked away, quickly disappearing into the crowd.

Judith made her way back to the car park in Jervis Street, confused and upset by the changes in Spider and his reactions to her. This wasn't the way it was supposed to be. In the terrible weeks following the accident, when she had woken screaming from the nightmares in which she had relived the crash again and again, it had been thoughts of Spider which had comforted her. And when the police had arrived, asking her the same questions which her father had asked: what was he like? what did he do? what did he say? where did he go? did he force you to go with him? did he hurt you? did he ever ask for money? she had told them nothing, absolutely nothing, feeling that she was protecting Spider, keeping him safe.

When she had been sent back to boarding school, she knew it was simply to keep her away from Spider. She knew that in some strange way, her father, immensely powerful and wealthy, was somehow afraid of Spider. She had started reading the papers, looking for any mention of travellers and itinerants, hoping that it might give her a clue to Spider's whereabouts.

She had dreamt about meeting up with Spider again. Today the dream had come true. And she was almost sorry it had.

Reality wasn't like the dream. Judith remembered Spider as tall and handsome, dark and daring, whereas now she saw him as simply another skinny boy, dark greasy hair pulled back into a ridiculous pony tail, dirty skin, calloused hands, badly in need of a bath. Had he changed so much ... or had she?

Crossing O'Connell Bridge she spotted a woman crouched in against the stone balustrade. She was sitting on a square of cardboard, wrapped in a fringed blanket, a plastic butter box on the ground in front of her. As she drew closer, Judith was appalled when she discovered that the woman had a baby with her, wrapped up in the blanket.

'Spare some change, love?'

She was almost ashamed of herself when she walked on without stopping. Spider had told her that itinerant women sometimes borrowed babies when they went begging. But he had also taught her to look beyond the obvious: this was the only way the woman had of making money. If she was dirty it was because she had no access to hot running water. If she was wrapped in bulky clothing, it was simply to keep warm. But people never thought of that: they simply saw a woman begging on the bridge with a baby in her arms.

Judith crossed Bachelor's Walk and moments later turned left down Abbey Street, heading back to the car. She didn't see the two men squat down on either side of the woman begging on the bridge. Had she done so she might have recognised them as the two who had been chasing Spider.

~

'It's her all right,' Kathleen Ryan said triumphantly, her bright green eyes glittering. 'I'd recognise her anywhere.' She rocked the baby to and fro, gently soothing it, her eyes automatically checking over the people who passed by. She knew instinctively those who would give and those who would simply ignore her. Tourists were always a good mark, but there weren't many tourists around at this time of year.

'What happened, Da?' she asked the older man.

The squat balding man pulled a crumpled Marlboro packet from his pocket and shook out a bent cigarette which he stuck between his thin lips. He lit it up from a cheap disposable lighter of the kind he sometimes sold on Henry Street — four for a pound — when he needed to make a few bob. Holding the cigarette in nicotine-stained fingers, he picked a flake of tobacco from his top lip. 'We had him.' His accent was a typical traveller accent: broad and rural. 'We had him,' he repeated, 'and then the girl appeared. She screamed. He broke free. Gave me a good kicking on my leg too,' he added bitterly. He pulled up his trouser leg to show his scraped shin.

'And he kicked me in the knee,' Jed, Kathleen's older brother said, patting the leg that was stretched out in front of him. 'Damn near broke it.'

'You let him get away,' the girl snapped. 'The two of you couldn't hold him.'

'He got lucky,' Joe Ryan said, sucking smoke deep into his lungs. A police car drove across the bridge and the older man turned to follow it, staring hard at the two police officers, almost daring them to stop and say something to him.

'I followed them,' Jed said, breaking the long silence. Since their mother had died three years previously, Kathleen Ryan had taken on her role and had become almost unbearably domineering and demanding. She was the youngest child, and was still the apple of her father's eye — always had been, always would — and he backed up with his fists what she told her older brothers to do. After a while, obeying her became something of a habit.

'Where did they go? Did they see you?' Kathleen demanded.

'They did not,' Jed said indignantly. 'They headed up Grafton Street and had a meal in a burger place.' His own stomach rumbled loudly, reminding him that it was a long time since the cup of tea he'd had for breakfast.

'Had they met before?' Kathleen asked.

Jed shook his head. 'I don't think so. They seemed like people meeting for the first time in ages. They did a lot of talking, and at one point he got up and I thought he was going to leave. But he sat down again.'

'Then what happened?'

'They came out of the restaurant — she paid, by the way — and came back down Grafton Street. He stopped to give Crazy Kevin a couple of pence. They stood at the end of the street, in plain sight of two shades....' Jed stopped, shaking his head, remembering how close Spider had been to the police. 'Aye, but he's a cool customer all right. Then they split up; she headed back this way, while he went off down Nassau Street. But don't worry, Mickser is following him. He won't lose him.'

Kathleen nodded. She hadn't been chasing Spider across the country only to lose him again. 'Your brother better not lose him,' she said balefully.

~

The same sixth sense that had always kept him out of trouble had been nagging at him ever since he stepped out of the restaurant with Judith. The small hairs on the back of his neck were itching as if someone were staring at him, but he didn't want to risk turning around and giving the game away. When he'd spotted Crazy Kevin, he'd used the excuse of giving him money to take a quick glance behind him.

He'd immediately spotted Mickser and Jed Ryan on either side of the street, their bright red hair making them hard to miss. Both were staring hard into shop windows, hoping they wouldn't be spotted. Spider bit the inside of his cheek to keep a straight face: Mickser was looking at a window display of kitchen utensils, while Jed was standing before a window of women's lingerie. A couple strolled past and laughed loudly at the serious expression on his face. Jed suddenly realised what he was looking at and his cheeks bloomed bright red in embarrassment.

When he left Judith at the bottom of Grafton Street, Spider turned to the right into Nassau Street, then right again up Dawson Street. Moving quickly now, not daring to looking back in case they were behind him, he ducked into a bookshop. He was aware of the staff watching him closely as he moved through the shop, taking the short cut that led back into Creation Arcade in Grafton Street. He stood at Golden Discs where he could keep an eye on Grafton Street and the Arcade at the same time, looking for the Ryans' distinctive bright red hair. But he wasn't followed; he'd shaken them off.

Spider breathed deeply. He had stomach cramps from the food and all he wanted to do was to lie down and sleep. Judith was right. If he could rest for a couple of hours he'd be able to put together a plan. When you were on the run, constantly looking over your shoulder, trying to work out where your next meal was coming from, where you were going to spend the night, there simply wasn't time for anything else.

Almost unconsciously, he murmured the address Judith had given him.

3

He wasn't going to come, Judith finally admitted to herself. She looked at the clock on the kitchen wall. Ten past seven; five minutes since the last time she'd looked at it.

He wasn't going to come.

Why should he? She'd done nothing but cause him trouble. She'd destroyed his whole way of life. It was solely because of her that the police were looking for him; it was her fault that Kathleen's brothers were chasing him.

It was funny; since meeting him earlier that afternoon, she'd felt ... different. Changed. 'I don't love you,' he had said. The words hadn't sunk in then, hadn't made sense. He had told her he loved her. He had written her that note. *I love you.* Had he been lying then ... or was he lying now?

Confused, Judith shook her head. Spider was many things, but he was not a liar. No, he had simply been exhausted, and when people were tired they said things they didn't mean. He did love her. She knew he did!

Judith looked at the clock again. She would give him five more minutes ....

The front door bell chimed.

Her heart was thundering as she raced down the smoothly polished hall, sliding in her stockinged feet. Mindful of her parents' warning about answering the door, she checked through the peephole first. She could see no-one through the distorting circle of glass. She had heard the bell ... or had it been her imagination? Judith slipped the chain, pulled opened the front door and stepped out into the bitterly cold January night. There was no-one there. 'Spider?' she called, her breath puffing whitely on the air before her. 'Spider?'

Judith stepped back inside as her teeth began to chatter. It had been her imagination. He wasn't coming, she decided angrily, hurrying back into the kitchen. She'd clear up here and head back down to Peggy's house.

Judith was rinsing out the teapot when the face appeared at the window.

The scream caught at the back of her throat and the teapot crashed into the sink, shattering into a dozen pieces. She snapped on the exterior lights, flooding the patio and carefully landscaped rear garden in cold white light. The figure of a man spun around as he was caught in the lights. She was about to press the panic button which was connected to the local police station when she realised it was Spider standing on the glittering flagstones.

Judith wrenched open the patio doors. Cold air gusted into the kitchen.'You idiot,' she hissed, as Spider hurried inside.'I nearly called the police. Was that you at the front door a moment ago?' she continued. Spider nodded, his teeth chattering uncontrollably, unable to speak. Beneath the grime his face was deathly pale, and his hands were tucked deep into his armpits for warmth.

'You're freezing,' Judith realised. 'Here, come and stand by the radiator.' She touched his leather jacket, wincing at the chill it exuded. 'I'd just about given up on you,' she added.

Spider warmed his hands over the radiator. 'It's a long walk up here from town,' he said finally. 'The paths are icy.' He lifted his left leg, showing torn jeans and a bloody knee. 'I fell. After that, I was forced to slow down.'

Judith hurried about, making tea. She punched the timer on the microwave, and the pizza she'd made earlier began to spin slowly. 'It'll be a few minutes.'

Now that he could feel his fingers again, Spider unzipped his leather jacket and pulled out sheets of newspaper which he'd wrapped around his chest. He saw Judith staring at him. 'They keep out the chill,' he shrugged. He draped his jacket over the back of a high-backed kitchen chair, while he looked around the room.

The kitchen was enormous. It had been decorated in white and silver, and the overall effect was cool and functional. There was every conceivable kitchen appliance in the room and the walls were lined with white presses, spice racks, a tall wine rack, knife and other implement holders. The oval shaped kitchen table was polished white wood. There was a small colour television on the worktop. He suddenly recalled his parents' tiny kitchen. You could stand in the centre of the room and touch all four walls. When his father had finally managed to save enough to buy a washing machine and fridge, there was no longer any room for the whole family to eat in the kitchen.

But he'd known whole families who lived in spaces smaller than this kitchen.

He'd always realised Judith Meredith was wealthy — her father was supposedly one of the richest men in Ireland — but it was only as he tramped up Killiney Hill looking for the address that he began to have some idea of just how affluent the family must be. The house was set back off the road, behind a high wall and tall wrought-iron gates. Spider had climbed over the wall and dropped down into the darkened garden beyond, wincing as his knee troubled him. A house of this size was certainly protected by security devices. He'd circled the house twice, looking for any signs of activity, other than the lights in the kitchen. From the bottom of the garden he could see Judith sitting at the kitchen table, flicking through a magazine. She seemed to be alone. He'd finally rung the front door bell and then darted back into the bushes, watching while Judith opened the door and called his name. When he was satisfied that she was alone in the house, he'd gone back around to the back door and had been just about to knock when the garden lights had come on, blinding him.

The microwave pinged, and he looked up suddenly. Judith was staring at him. 'Why don't you go and wash?' she suggested. 'There's a bathroom through there.' She pointed to the kitchen door before turning back to the microwave.

Spider wandered out into the hall. The floor was cool marble, the staircase highly polished wood. There were more pictures on the walls than he'd ever seen in his life. The first door he peeked into was a cupboard; it was in darkness, but he could smell the chemical odours of polish and varnish. The second door was the bathroom.

Like the kitchen, the room was enormous, gleaming white tiles with a huge mirror over a deep sink. There was a toilet against one wall and a shower stall against the other. Pots of hideous cacti lined the window ledge. Spider shook his head, silently reminding himself that a house of this size would have two or more toilets. He scrubbed at his filthy hands with a bar of lemon-scented soap, then quickly washed his face. He was shocked at his reflection in the mirror; with his pasty skin, deep-sunk eyes and hollow cheeks, he looked like a junkie.

The sink was a mess when he'd finished, black and greasy soap-streaks staining the sparkling enamel. He wiped it clean with his hands, then dampened his metal comb and dragged it through his hair. It needed a wash. When he used one of the thick fluffy towels, he left black handprints on it.

'Spider?' Judith called from the kitchen.

She was pouring soup when he came back into the kitchen, the room warm and rich with its odour. 'This will warm you up,' she said as he sat before the table.

'Thanks ... I ....'

'Eat first, then we'll talk.' She was confident now. He had come, and he was now on her territory, in her world, where she knew the rules. She sat opposite him, watching while he ate the soup quickly, cleaning the bowl with thick slices of French bread. She saw him blink in astonishment as she laid a large pizza before him.

'You made this?' he asked, cutting a thick triangular slice and lifting it with his fingers.

She shrugged. 'Yes. But it's not as hard as it looks. The bases are ready-made, and so is the sauce; all I had to do was to add the topping.'

When he had finished, she poured a steaming mug of tea and pushed the milk and sugar towards him.

Spider slumped back in the chair and smiled. 'I feel human again.'

'You look better,' she said. 'I nearly didn't recognise you today.'

Spider put his elbows on the table and leaned across.'Why did you come after me today?'

Judith smiled, her teeth white and perfect. 'I've spent the last six months hoping I'd hear from you. When I spotted you in Henry Street, I couldn't believe my eyes. And then when I saw you run through the arcade followed by the red-haired guy, I knew you were in trouble. I couldn't walk away.'

Spider nodded, satisfied with the answer. Exhaustion washed over him in a long slow wave and he felt his eyelids droop. He was hot and his stomach was full: he hadn't felt this good in a long time.

'Would they have hurt you?' she asked softly.

He shrugged. 'They would. First we stole their van, then wrecked it. They want to be paid for that, for a start ....'

'But the insurance ....'

Spider snorted rudely.'It wasn't insured. Where do you think two young travellers of no fixed abode are going to find insurance? Since they knew I'd no money to give them, they were going to get some satisfaction by beating me up.'

Judith quickly tried to work out how much money she had in her bank account, and how she could get it all out without her father learning about it. 'If I gave you the money for the van ...' she began.

Spider shook his head. 'No! They're getting nothing out of me. Even if I had the money I wouldn't give it to them.' A sudden yawn took him by surprise. 'Sorry. It's the heat and the food.'

Judith glanced up at the clock. It was close to nine. She stood up. 'I'd better be going anyway, or Peggy will send a search party up here. She knows I'm studying for my exams, but I've got to sleep over in her house.'

Spider stood up too, feeling unsure. Was she asking him to leave? She had said he could stay, but he thought that might have just been in the heat of the moment, and she was hardly likely to leave a total stranger in her home.

'I've made up the bed in the guest room,' Judith continued, walking out into the hall and hurrying upstairs. 'Its at the back of the house, so no lights will show.'

Spider followed her out into the hall and up the stairs.

'Bathroom and toilet are here,' she pointed out the doors, 'and your room is here.'

Spider followed her into the bedroom. It had been decorated in soft pastel pinks, salmon and rose, with matching carpets and eiderdown. It was spotless, and he felt dirty just standing there. There was a pair of black jeans across the end of the bed.

'I hope they're your size,' Judith said, suddenly embarrassed. She had never bought a present for a boy before.

Without a word, Spider lifted the jeans — Levi's, not the usual cheap jeans he bought himself — and checked the label. Thirty waist, thirty-three leg. 'They'll fit,' he said simply, and was about to say more, when the phone rang, startling them both.

'Peggy probably,' Judith said. She took the call in her parents' bedroom. When she returned to the room, Spider was standing exactly where she had left him. 'That was Peggy. It's starting to snow, and she wants me to come down to the house now. I said I was on the way.' She stopped, unsure of what to say. She wanted to ask him if he would be there in the morning. 'Look, make yourself at home. The heating is on; the water is hot if you want a bath. If the phone rings, ignore it; the answering machine will take the call. I'll be back early in the morning.'

She was turning away when Spider said, 'And you're just leaving me here?'

'Yes.'

'Do you trust me that much?'

'I trust you.'

Spider followed her down the stairs and waited while she shrugged on her heavy coat. 'Does anyone know I'm here?'

Judith shook her head. 'No-one.'

~

The newspaper cutting was yellowed and frayed. Kathleen Ryan spread it out on the caravan table, holding down the folding edges with a salt cellar and a sugar bowl. It was cold in the caravan, even though the gas fire had been burning all night, but the chill night air seeped in under the ill-fitting doors and through crooked windows. She tapped the grainy newspaper photograph with a ragged fingernail. 'Is that the girl?'

Mickser nodded quickly. 'That's her. Pretty ... but skinny,' he added hurriedly, seeing the expression in his sister's hard green eyes.

'It says here her Da is Maxwell Meredith, a rich man, a very rich man with an address in Killiney.' The flame-haired young woman squinted as the uncertain battery light flickered. 'Who do we know works the Killiney area?' she asked, looking across at her father and older brother.

Jed shrugged. 'Killiney's not a good area. Too rich,' he added with a gap-toothed grin. It was always the poor who gave; those who could least afford it.

'Why the sudden interest in Killiney?' Mickser asked.

Kathleen fought to control her fiery temper. 'Because the girl's from Killiney. And Spider's disappeared off the streets. Can you not put two and two together?'

'So what's she going to do?' Jed asked derisively. 'Invite him into her home. What's Mammy and Daddy going to say about that, eh? Look, Kitty, let him go, forget about him. He's not worth it.'

'You tell him, Da,' Kathleen spat.

Joe Ryan looked up from the flickering screen of the small portable black and white television. 'Your brother's right,

Kitty. We should let this go. Concentrate on our own business.'

Kathleen put her hands on her hips and glared at the three men. 'He humiliated the two of you,' she said icily to Jed and Mickser. 'He made me look a fool in front of my own people for a spoilt little rich girl. Then he stole our van and smashed it up. But Spider didn't spend any time with the police, did he? No, you did. Are you going to forget about that?'

Jed raised his hands in surrender at the verbal onslaught. 'All right. All right. So, we owe him ... and he owes us.' He had spent the best part of three days in police custody answering questions about his van which had been used to ram a police road-block. He claimed it had been stolen, but that he had never got around to reporting the theft. The police clearly didn't believe him but, without any evidence, they had been forced to let him go. 'What do you want us to do?' he asked eventually.

'I want you to find out where Miss Judith Meredith lives in Killiney. Then we'll go and ask her where we can find Spider.'

'Do you think she knows?' Mickser asked.

'I'm convinced of it.'

'But will she tell us?' he wondered.

'She'll tell me,' Kathleen assured him.

Sunday 17th January

4

Spider's parents had been travellers, but before he was born they had given up the road, determined to give him the chance of a way of life they had never known. As a boy he had grown up in a succession of small terraced houses, first in Cabra, then Crumlin and finally Finglas. They had been happy times, and the houses always seemed to be filled with either his mother's or father's large family of brothers and sisters. He would creep out of bed and crouch on the stairs listening to the stories they told of the open road.

But when he ran away for the first time, determined to have his own adventures and to escape the routine boredom of school and home, he discovered that life as a runaway wasn't as attractive and adventurous as he had heard. People tended only to remember the good times, the long hot summers, the open road stretching on forever with enough work in the farms and houses to keep body and soul together. They never spoke about the winters, when the rain seeped through every corner of a caravan, when there was no work, no money, and often no place to stop as locals moved travellers on, unwilling to allow them to stay even one night, fearing that they might settle in.

As he became more experienced, Spider learned to enjoy the freedom of travelling, of living by his wits, of being responsible to no-one but himself. It was only after Judith had come along that he realised just how aimless his life had been ... and how selfish.

But now that he'd been on the run for six months, he'd begun to yearn for the simple way of life again.

However, Spider admitted, there were certain advantages of living in a house — like hot running water. He would be eighteen years old next birthday, at the end of September, but he could actually count on the fingers of one hand the number of baths he'd had in the previous five years. He'd had showers of course. Some of the halting sites had showers and so too did one or two of the bigger caravans, but he hadn't come across anyone with a bath in their caravan. He'd always taken special pride in his appearance. The black leather jacket, tee-shirt, cowboy boots and jeans 'look' was one he specially cultivated, and his thick black hair looked really well pulled back off his face and tied into a ponytail. He had always been clean; his hair was always spotless, he was clean-shaven and he used deodorants. But that had been before the craziness of last summer. He'd scraped together enough money to buy himself a second-hand van, which had been his home. When he'd been forced to abandon it when Kathleen and her brothers had attacked him he'd lost everything. He'd got his own back though, when he'd taken their van. He smiled quickly. The last time he'd seen that van it had been a bullet-riddled hulk. He'd been running ever since, not eating properly, sleeping only when he could, washing himself with freezing rain or river water. He didn't mind not eating, and he could get by on a couple of hours sleep, but he hated being dirty, he hated the bitter odour of his own stale sweat.

He'd eaten well today though, there was a warm bed waiting for him, and right now he was looking forward to a long hot bath.

Spider stood in the centre of the gleaming bathroom and listened to the hot water thunder into the enormous tub. He added lemon-scented bubble bath to the water, then watched in alarm as a profusion of frothy bubbles threatened to spill out on to the floor. Spinning the taps furiously, he turned the water off. He tested the water with his hand, added some more cold water, then slowly ... slowly ... slowly sank down into the bath. Taking a deep breath and squeezing his eyes shut, he dunked his head beneath the surface, hearing the water roar in his ears. He sat up spluttering, brushing water from his eyes.

This was heaven!

Suddenly he ached. Tired muscles began to protest as the hot water seeped into them. He worked his head from side to side, easing the stiffness in his neck. Sitting up in the bath, Spider scrubbed himself all over with a bar of white odourless soap. Within ten minutes the water was scummed with grey, and he pulled the plug, letting the water gurgle away, leaving a grey tide mark around the edge of the bath. He washed it away, cleaned out the bath, and then refilled it, lying back while the water rose up around him, cooler now, but much more pleasant.

Without the ever-present tensions of the streets, Spider allowed himself to relax. He hadn't felt this good in ... well, in a long time. There were, he knew, very few times in his life when he had ever been truly happy. Content, yes, but never happy.

He had been happy last summer though.

Spider nodded unconsciously. Last summer, when he had met Judith Meredith, had been one of the happiest times in his life. Sometimes, when he was deeply depressed, he hated Judith, hated what she had done to him, hated all the pain and hurt she had caused him. And yet, when she had appeared today, when he could have simply run past her and vanished into the Saturday afternoon crowd, he had grabbed her arm and hauled her away with him.

He had told her he didn't love her. He had said that it had all been a lie. It wasn't. When he'd seen her today, he realised that he was still very much in love with her.

~

Spider woke with a start.

For a single moment he panicked as he looked around the bright, cheerful and completely alien bedroom. He didn't know where he was. Then the events of the previous day slid back into place and he knew he was lying in bed in Judith's house, warm, comfortable and relaxed.

Easing himself up on his elbows, he found Judith sitting on the end of the bed, a tray held before her. In the cool morning light, without make-up and with her hair tied back in a ponytail, she looked younger than her fifteen years.

'I didn't mean to wake you,' she lied. She had been sitting watching him sleep a whole ten minutes. His face was different in repose, younger, smoother. He had washed and shaved, and his jet-black hair gleamed. She noticed how pale his skin was, and how long and dark his eyelashes were against his face. But suddenly becoming embarrassed by her intense scrutiny of him, she had deliberately coughed aloud to waken him.

'You look better,' she said, as he sat up in bed. He was wearing a pair of her father's silk pyjamas, which were at least two sizes too big for him.

Spider ran his fingers through his loose hair, dragging it back off his face. 'I feel good,' he admitted. 'I haven't felt this rested or clean for months. What time is it?' he asked, watching as Judith pulled out the legs of the tray and snapped them into position. The tray sat on the bed across Spider's legs. There was a large pot of tea, a rack of toast with butter and marmalade, a bowl of corn flakes, milk, sugar and two thick earthenware mugs.

'It's close to eleven,' Judith said, glancing at her wrist-watch.

Spider poured milk over the corn flakes, then sprinkled them with sugar. It had been ten-thirty when he had turned out the light the previous night. He had slept for nearly twelve hours. As he munched through the big bowl of corn flakes, Judith began pulling clothes from a plastic bag.

'I've brought you a couple of my sailing jumpers,' she began.

'Your sailing jumpers?'

'During the summer I sail out of Dun Laoghaire,' she explained. 'Daddy has a small yacht.' She lifted out a heavy woollen jumper. 'It can get very cold on the boat so we have to wear warm clothing. This jumper is about three sizes too big for me, so I can wear it over a life-jacket. It should fit you.'

Spider looked at the jumper. It was enormous. It had been knitted from a thick tweed wool in an incredibly complicated Aran pattern. It even looked warm ... and he guessed it was expensive.

'I've also brought you some of my extra-large tee-shirts. I hope they fit.' She held up two black tee-shirts emblazoned with the Guns 'N Roses logo. 'And some socks,' she added. 'I wear them when I'm sailing and riding, and they're very big on me.'

Spider finally managed to break in. 'But you can't go giving me all these clothes,' he protested.

'Why not?'

'Because ... because what happens when you need them again?'

'I won't be needing them for ages, and then I'll ask Daddy to buy some more,' she said simply, and in that instant, she highlighted the differences that lay between the two of them more starkly than any other display of her wealth. Spider had never been in a position to buy without thinking. Before he made a single purchase, he knew exactly how much it would cost, how much he had in his pocket and how much he would have left when he was finished.

'I'll get out of your way today,' he said, not looking at her as he poured two cups of tea.

'You don't have to go,' Judith said quickly.

Spider grinned, his dark eyes sparkling. 'Well, I can't stay here, can I? What would your parents say?'

Judith had no answer to that. Last night she had been pleased and excited that Spider had come, but this morning she had woken full of worries again. What if he had vanished during the night? And then that nasty, insidious thought had slid into the back of her mind: what if he had gone and had cleaned out the house too? She had lain on her pillow and shaken her head fiercely; Spider wouldn't do that.

But all the same, she had been relieved when she had arrived and discovered that all he'd done was have a bath and then climb into bed.

'When are your parents back?' Spider continued.

'Tomorrow night,' she said quietly. 'You could stay until then.'

He nodded.

'Where will you go?' Judith asked into the long silence that followed.

Spider chewed toast, leaning over the tray so as not to dribble crumbs on to the bed. 'I was thinking I might go to England,' he said eventually. 'There's nothing for me here,' he continued, not seeing the sudden look of hurt in Judith's big brown eyes. 'I might be able to get a job, save enough to buy a van, and start back out on the road again.'

'What about Kathleen and her brothers?' Judith asked. She hadn't touched the tea Spider had poured for her.

'If I stay away long enough they'll end up in jail,' he said confidently.

'Why?' she asked, surprised.

'They've always been petty thieves. They'll get caught sooner or later.' He added more sugar to his tea. 'If I go away now, I could come back in a few years with a new name, a new identity. Maybe the police would have forgotten about me by then.'

Judith folded and unfolded the tee-shirts in her hands, finally throwing them on the bed. 'Would you stay if we could clear your name?'

He shrugged. 'I might. I wouldn't have a reason for leaving.'

'But what about Kathleen?' Judith asked.

The phone rang.

The sound shocked them both motionless, then Judith reached for the phone beside Spider's bed. 'Probably my parents,' she said. 'Now be quiet.' She picked up the phone on the third ring, just before the answering machine cut in. 'Hello?'

There was silence on the other end of the line.

'Hello?'

'Judith Meredith?' The voice was a hoarse whisper, but Judith detected an accent similar to Spider's.

'Yes; who is this?' she asked, crouching down by the side of the bed and turning the phone so that Spider could listen in.

'You know where Spider O'Brien is.' It was a statement, not a question. 'You should tell us.' The phone went dead.

Spider leaned over, gently took the phone from Judith's hands and replaced it on its cradle.

'How did they find you?' Judith asked in a whisper.

'They didn't,' Spider said. He sat up in bed and drew his knees up to his chest, wrapping his arms around his shins. 'If they knew where I was they wouldn't have bothered phoning. They probably recognised you yesterday and assumed you and I were together.'

The phone shrilled again.

Judith snatched it up. 'Who are you? What do you want?'

'Spider O'Brien. Tell us where he is.'

'I don't know.'

'Don't lie to me.' The hoarseness went from the voice, leaving it recognisably female. 'You were seen with him. Tell us where he is.'

'I'm going to phone the police,' Judith snapped, a sudden surge of anger flowing through her when she realised that she was frightened.

'I don't think you will, Judith Meredith. The police are still looking for your boyfriend. You don't want to get him into any more trouble now, do you?'

Judith hung up.

Spider threw back the covers and slipped out of bed. 'I'd better get dressed. I'd say they're close by. Probably watching the house. If the phone rings again, don't answer it.'

The phone rang again.

~

Kathleen slammed the phone down. She had been going to leave a message on the answering machine, but had decided against it. It would be better to leave no evidence, nothing that could be taken to the police. She stamped out of the phone booth and climbed into the battered red Toyota Corolla.

'I spoke to her twice,' she said to Jed and Mickser. 'But now she's turned on an answering machine. She's in the house all right.'

Mickser leaned in over the back seat of the car. 'What would you have done if her parents had answered?'

'Put on my best posh accent and asked for Judith,' Kathleen said, brilliantly mimicking an upper-class Dublin accent. She tapped her older brother on the shoulder. 'Give me twenty pence,' she said with a grin. 'I want to make another phone call.'

5

Spider suddenly swore and jerked away from the bedroom window.

Judith said nothing. The expression on his face — ice cold, angry — was enough to tell her that they were in trouble. 'Shades,' he said tersely. 'Police.'

'But how...?' she whispered, as she darted towards the window and peered out. A police car was cruising slowly up the long drive. 'Kathleen,' she answered herself.

'Kathleen,' Spider whispered, nodding fiercely.

'Stay here,' she said firmly. 'I'll handle this.'

Spider nodded again. He waited until Judith had slipped from the room, then hurried back to the window. This time he looked beyond the garden into the road. The day was grey and overcast; dark, lowering clouds seeming to hug the tree tops. Although it was nearly noon, the street lights were still on. He knew it would snow before the day was out.

Spider spotted the car immediately. It was a dark red Toyota Corolla, its bonnet and doors eaten with rust, completely out of place in this affluent neighbourhood. He was able to make out three occupants as it drove slowly past, pale white ovals of faces peering in the direction of the house through the misted-up windows. His hands closed into tight fists. He didn't think there was any way that Kathleen and her brothers could know where he was; they were simply playing a game with Judith. No doubt when the police had left there would be another phone call or two.

Spider moved back to the bedroom door and cracked it open a fraction. The voices from the hall below drifted up clearly.

'You are Miss Judith Meredith?'

'Yes, Garda.'

'We came as soon as we could, miss.' The voice was male, with a strong Cork accent. 'What seems to be the problem?'

'I didn't call you.'

There was a long pause, then another male voice — an older man, a Dublin accent — said, 'Could we speak to your parents, Miss Meredith?'

'My parents are away,' Judith said forcefully. 'Now would you mind telling me what this is all about?'

Spider clearly heard the older man sigh. 'We got a call seven minutes ago from you ....'

'Not from me,' Judith interrupted.

'From Miss Judith Meredith, this address, this phone number. You said,' he paused and Spider guessed that he was reading, '... you said that there was a prowler in the grounds. You identified the prowler as Seán O'Brien, the young man who abducted you last year.'

Spider gripped the door frame tightly. Very few people outside of the travelling community knew that his real name was Seán. He also realised just how clever Kathleen had been. There were just enough elements of truth in the lie to make the police interested, and no matter what Judith said, it would seem like a lie.

'I did not phone the police. There have been no prowlers. And, for your information, Seán O'Brien did not abduct me last year. I went willingly with him.'

'I'm sure you did, miss. Perhaps we could speak to your parents?'

'I've already told you that my parents are away for the weekend,' Judith snapped, angered by the tone of condescension in the police officer's voice.

Spider silently shook his head. Wrong answer.

'Then you wouldn't object if we had a look around, miss?'

'I most certainly would. I did not phone you, officer. I made no report. So there is no reason for you to be here.'

Spider shook his head again; taking that tone with the police would get her nowhere. They were responding to what they thought was a genuine call. Now, their time had been wasted and they were getting lip from a stuck-up teenager.

'You realise that making a hoax call to the police is a serious offence, Miss Meredith.' The Corkman's accent had turned hard. 'We can very easily check to see if a call has been made from this house.'

'Well, why don't you do that!' Moments later the front door slammed.

When Judith raced back upstairs and into the bedroom, Spider was standing by the window, peering down at the two officers sitting in the blue car. Spider held up a hand, silently warning Judith to keep back.

'What's happening?' she asked, her voice trembling now, the realisation that she had just stood up to two police officers beginning to sink in.

'They're on the radio. I would imagine they're making a report.'

'Kathleen made the phone call, didn't she?' Judith asked.

Spider nodded. 'She phoned the police pretending to be you. I imagine we'll be hearing from her soon.' He turned to glance at Judith, his lips twisted into a wry smile. 'You realise of course, that if *you* phone the police, they won't be so quick to respond.'

Judith nodded, not sure what Spider was getting at.

'I think Kathleen might be planning a visit here,' he said very softly. 'You shouldn't be here if that happens.'

'She wouldn't dare come here.'

'She might,' he murmured. 'They've been chasing me for a long time. They're not likely to give up a chance to discover my whereabouts.'

'But why, Spider? Everything that happened between you and her, happened last year. Why can't they let that be? Why are they hounding you?'

The young man turned away from the window. His shrug was almost lost under the heavy tweed jumper. 'Because they lost face. It's difficult to explain, Judith, but us travellers live by a very strict code. Our word is our bond. There are no written contracts on the road. Men have lived and traded for generations on a handshake and a promise. Nothing more was needed.' He took a deep breath, then held up his hand and began ticking off points. 'I shamed Kathleen in front of the other travellers, in front of her family, friends and neighbours.' A second finger. 'Then we stole their van ...' — third finger — 'and wrecked it...' — his little finger '... and I haven't paid for it. Any one of those reasons would be enough to cause a feud between us. But all four....' He didn't finish the sentence.

'How can it be stopped?' Judith demanded as Spider brushed past her and out on to the landing.

He stopped on the stairs, and looked back up at her. 'It's gone too far to be stopped. If they caught up with me, and gave me a good beating, that might satisfy their honour. But they haven't had much success in that department either,' he added with a grin. He continued on down the stairs.

After a moment's hesitation, Judith followed him. She found him in the kitchen, filling the kettle with water.

'Could we pay them?' she asked.

Spider considered for a moment, his black eyes staring out into the back garden. During the summer it would be a riot of colour, but now, in the depths of winter it was flat and drab, skeletal bushes and bare earth. He shook his head. 'I think it's gone beyond money. They're looking for revenge.'

Judith ran both hands through her blond hair and threw her head back. This was a nightmare! And it was getting out of control. Feuds, vendettas ... things like that didn't happen in the world she lived in. In her world, she was accustomed to money taking care of everything. Last year, when she'd run away for a week, Daddy had paid for the damage to the police cars, and because Daddy was so wealthy and a close personal friend of a lot of politicians, the police were reluctant to make too much of his daughter's involvement in the case. Also, she knew that Daddy's position — and his many friends — had ensured that much of the story never reached the newspapers.

The phone rang.

Judith snatched it up before the answering machine could cut in and take the message. 'Who is this?'

'I hope you were nice to the policemen.' This time there was no attempt made to disguise the voice, and Judith recognised Kathleen immediately.

'Why did you do that?' Judith demanded. Spider came around the table and put his ear to the phone, his jet black hair mingling with her blond hair, tickling her cheek.

'Just to prove to you that I can make your life very miserable.'

'What do you want?' Judith struggled to keep her voice under control.

'I want Spider, or do you call him Seán? I suppose a well brought up girl like you would call him by his proper name.'

'I don't know where Spider is,' Judith lied.

The voice at the other end of the line turned hard and sharp. 'I think you do. You were seen with him yesterday. The pair of you had a nice little chat over lunch. I want to know what you talked about. I want to know where he is.'

'I hadn't seen him in six months,' Judith said desperately.

'Don't lie to me,' Kathleen snapped.

'It's not a lie! I met him by chance yesterday. I bought him some food. That's it. He went his way. I went mine. I don't expect ever to see him again.'

'And you expect me to believe that? You're lying to me, and do you know how I know you're lying? Because you never said you gave him money. If you knew you weren't going to be seeing him again, you would have given him money. But you didn't. Which means you are either still seeing him or you are going to see him soon. Maybe he's even going to come and visit you. Perhaps I should come over to your place and wait for him. That would be a nice surprise, wouldn't it? His ex-girlfriend and his current girlfriend in the one room. What a choice he'd have?'

'I was never his girlfriend ....'

'What were you then?'

'We were friends ....'

'Friends?' Kathleen made the word sound obscene. 'Yes, I think I should come over there ....'

'I'll phone the police,' Judith said.

'And what do you think they'll say to another call from Miss Judith Meredith? What's that story called ... oh yes, the boy who cried wolf. Now you can save yourself a lot of misery by simply telling me where's he's staying.'

'I don't know.'

'I think you do.'

'It's true,' Judith insisted.

'I don't believe you,' Kathleen spat and hung up.

As Judith replaced the receiver, Spider wandered back to the kettle and switched it off. When he turned around his face was set into a determined mask. 'We better get out of here if Kathleen and her brothers are coming over.'

'Why can't we just stay here? We'll be safe. They cannot get in.'

'They don't have to get in. All they have to do is sit outside and wait for you to leave. We should get out now; I'll go with you as far as your sister-in-laws. You'll be safe there.'

'What about you? What will you do? Where will you go?'

'I'll think of something.'

~

'I'm sure she's alone in the house,' Kathleen said, her green eyes flashing excitedly.

'Why?' Mickser asked.

'Because she dealt with the police herself. If her mother or father had been there, they would have come to the door. Also, she's answered all my calls.' Kathleen rubbed her hand across the car window and squinted at the house that was just visible through the bare branches of the trees. 'Why don't we give her a call?'

'But you said the answering machine was on,' Mickser said slowly.

'I meant in person, you idiot.'

Her brother shook his head doubtfully. 'I don't know.'

Kathleen, who was sitting in the back seat, punched him hard in the shoulder. 'I wasn't asking for your opinion; I was telling you what we were going to do.'

6

'Come on.' Spider watched as Judith pulled on her boots. 'We don't have much time. They could be here any minute.'

'I hate running away from them,' Judith grumbled.

'Run away and live to fight another day,' Spider sang softly.

'I still think we're safer here,' Judith protested. 'Anyway, they don't know I'm here on my own.'

Spider shook his head. 'They do. They've been watching the house. They drove past as you were talking to the police. You've answered all Kathleen's calls.'

Pulling his hair back, he wrapped an elastic band around it, making a neat ponytail. It was only when Judith saw him looking at himself in the mirror that she realised he was probably quite vain about his appearance. He saw her watching him and shrugged in embarrassment. 'It keeps it out of the way,' he said, referring to his hair.

'I'm ready,' Judith said, slipping on a waxed green jacket. She pulled on a pair of thick woollen gloves.

Spider nodded. 'We'll go out the back way, and leave them watching the front.' He smiled. 'It's going to snow soon. Let them freeze in the car; it'll teach them a lesson.'

Judith followed Spider into the kitchen. First, he turned off the lights and then made Judith stand for a few moments until her eyes had adjusted to the dim light. 'Stay here,' he said softly. He crossed to the large windows and stared intently at the back garden, looking for anything unusual. When he was satisfied that there was no-one outside, he called Judith forward with a wave of his arm.

'I feel like a thief in my own house,' she whispered, and then said, 'Why am I whispering?'

'Sssh,' Spider hissed. 'Have you got your keys?' he asked.

Judith tapped her pocket.

Spider turned the key in the kitchen door and cracked it open slightly. Cold, damp air gusted into the room. 'All clear,' he murmured, stepping out into the back garden. Judith followed him, pulling the door closed behind her, then locking it securely. She didn't want her parents arriving home to find that the house had been burgled because she had left the back door open.

'This way.' Spider caught her hand and pulled her forward. She could feel the chill of his flesh through her thick woollen gloves, and suddenly realised she should have borrowed a pair of her father's gloves for him.

The Meredith house was situated on Killiney Hill, overlooking Killiney Bay. The long sloping rear garden ran down to a patio which was usually screened from the house by bushes and carefully tended shrubs. When Spider had been looking for a way into the gardens, he had discovered that the patio was actually quite close to the road, the usually impenetrable weave of bushes and trees having been stripped by winter, making it relatively easy to force a passage through.

The couple raced across the soggy back garden, Judith's boot heels sinking into the soft earth. The air was so cold it seared the girl's lungs, and she pulled her scarf up to cover her mouth and nose. They ran on to the patio — just as Mickser pushed his way through the bushes!

Spider didn't slow down. He hit the red-haired youth with his shoulder, sending him crashing back into the bushes. Off-balance, Mickser flailed around, becoming completely entangled in the heart of the bushes, bare thorny branches gripping his clothing with skeletal wooden fingers. He was so wrapped up in coat, scarf and hood that he couldn't call out properly, but his high-pitched grunts made his older brother poke his head through the hole in the bushes. 'Oh,' he breathed, finding Spider and Judith standing in front of him. Before he could react, however, Spider had caught him by the hood of his cheap anorak, twisting it savagely so that he couldn't cry out. Then he hauled him into the garden, and pushed him into the bushes on top of his brother. Spider planted one foot on top of Jed, forcing him down while he held the bushes apart for Judith. 'Quickly, quickly,' he urged.

She squeezed through the bushes, wincing as the twigs scratched at her face and left long scrape marks on her new coat. As she clambered over the wall, she spotted the red Toyota Corolla parked at the bottom of the road. Spider pulled himself free of the bushes and caught her hand. 'Let's go.'

Moments later, the Toyota started up after them.

~

Sergeant Tom Killeen tapped Garda Joe Collins on the shoulder. 'Swing back by the Meredith house, Joe. Something about the set-up there didn't ring right.'

The young Garda swung the wheel, bringing the car around in a tight half circle. 'Do you think she made the call to the station, Sarge?"

'Maybe. My own girl is about her age, and I know when she's up to something. And that Meredith girl was definitely up to something.'

'What exactly did the message say?' Garda Collins asked.

The sergeant consulted a clipboard on his lap. 'She said, and I quote, 'You've got to come quickly, there's someone in the garden. It's Seán O'Brien. He's come back for me. He's the one who abducted me last year. You've got to come.' He looked up from his notes. 'Now if it's a practical joke, it's an elaborate one.'

'Yet she denied making the call,' the driver reminded him.

The two men suddenly looked at each other. 'Unless she was forced to say that,' the sergeant whispered. 'Unless O'Brien was already in the house, threatening her ....'

The driver reached for the lights and siren switch, but the sergeant shook his head. 'Let's try to do this quietly.'

~

'Your sister-in-law's,' Spider panted, 'which direction?'

Judith jerked her thumb over her shoulder. 'Back there.'

He snatched a quick look back over his shoulder. Jed and Mickser were scrambling out of the hedge, trailing twigs and broken sticks. The red Toyota pulled alongside, its wheels skidding on the icy road. Jed wrenched open the passenger door and jumped inside, while Mickser took off after them at a run.

Spider and Judith turned to the left at the bottom of the hill, moving as quickly as possible on the slippery ground. Spider thought about darting into the driveway of one of the big houses, but all the gates were locked. There was a crash behind him as Kathleen's brother rounded the corner too quickly and his feet shot out from under him, dropping him heavily to the ground.

The couple turned to the left again, up a narrow road that was deeply shadowed from the two high walls on either side. Judith clung tightly to Spider's hand, feeling her feet shift on the icy path. At the top of the road, Spider stopped and glanced back. His breath was coming in great heaving gasps, and a deep wracking cough bent him double. When he straightened up, wiping the back of his hand across his watering eyes, he was surprised to find no-one following them.

'They're up to something,' he panted. 'They've probably left Mickser at the bottom of the road, while they're doubling around. We're trapped ...' he began, and then stopped. A car had turned into the road. In the dim afternoon light it was hard to make out any details.

~

Sergeant Tom Killeen leaned forward and pointed at the two figures standing on the side of the road. 'There,' he hissed. 'That's them.'

'He seems to be holding on to her Sarge ....'

The sergeant flipped on the lights and siren, impaling the couple in revolving blue and white lights. They remained motionless for a moment, then the youth pulled the girl away, dragging her into the darkness. The young Garda floored the accelerator, wheels spinning on the icy road, the car fishtailing until its tyres caught and it lurched forward. But by then the couple had vanished into the shadows. Sergeant Killeen reached for the radio. He was annoyed to discover that his hand was shaking. While he'd been talking to the girl at the door, the youth had obviously been close by. The boy must have intimidated her into saying nothing. God alone knows what he'd said or done when he discovered that she'd phoned the police. That was probably why he decided to take her away from the house.

Seán — Spider — O'Brien had escaped Garda custody once before. But he wouldn't escape so easily this time. Kidnapping was a very serious offence.

As the sergeant made his report, a battered red Toyota Corolla made its way slowly up the road. Two men and a women turned to looked at the police. The young constable noticed that they all had red hair.

7

Maxwell Meredith sat down on the edge of the bed and carefully replaced the phone. His wife, Frankie, came out of the bathroom wrapped in a thick white hotel towel, a second towel wrapped around her head. Steam curled from her damp flesh. 'Who was that?' she asked, and then stopped, knowing by the expression on her husband's face that something was terribly wrong.

'That was Peggy,' he said, his voice barely above a whisper. 'The police are with them at the moment ....'

'The police,' Frankie said quickly. 'Judith.'

Maxwell nodded. 'Judith. She's been abducted. The police say it's that boy she ran away with last year.'

Frankie sat down beside her husband and put a damp arm around his shoulder. 'Are you sure she's been abducted?' she asked quietly. Judith had done this before. On the day Francis Rourke-Heffernan had married Maxwell Meredith, Judith had simply walked away from the reception. The girl had come back a week later, older, wiser and sorry for the trouble and heartache she'd caused. Frankie had sat with Judith every day in the hospital, listening to her step-daughter tell — again and again — the story of her week's adventures. Frankie had realised then that Judith thought she was in love with the traveller. 'Maybe she has simply run off with him again,' she suggested cautiously.

Maxwell shook his head. 'She phoned the police in some distress, saying that the boy was prowling around the garden. The police sent a car up to the house, but she denied ever making the call. And do you know what they did then? They walked away and left her. A fifteen year old girl alone in the house, and they simply left her.'

'What was she doing alone in the house?' Frankie wondered, but Maxwell wasn't listening. If his daughter had been abducted, he was determined that someone would pay — starting with the two idiots in the patrol car. 'The police realise now that Spider was probably somewhere in the house, watching her,' he continued. 'They were seen shortly afterwards on one of the side roads; he was dragging her away with him.'

Frankie stood up pulled the towel off her blonde hair and began patting it dry. She was sure there was some mistake. From what Judith had told her, Spider wouldn't do anything to harm her; on the contrary, he had done everything to protect her. 'I'll start packing,' she said, walking back into the bathroom, slamming the door behind her. She stared at her reflection in the mirror and made a face. Judith seemed to specialise in ruining special occasions. Last year, it was the honeymoon; tonight they had been going to see the final performance of *Les Miserables*. It had taken her a year to get the tickets. She had been so looking forward to it.

8

When Spider was six years old he had brought home a dog, a tiny, wire-haired mongrel. That dog had caused him nothing but trouble and heartache. It had caught every disease going, lost an ear and most of its tail in a fight and was forever limping home with one or other of its legs injured. When it had eventually been run over he hadn't been sure whether to laugh or cry, although he realised later that the emotion he actually felt was relief. He had loved that dog, though there were times when he hated it, loathed it because it was nothing but trouble. But he always felt guilty when he shouted or swore at the dumb animal.

Now he was discovering that his feelings towards Judith Meredith were equally mixed.

Crouching beside the girl in a clump of damp bushes, Spider wondered how he had ended up in this situation. The girl was trouble; if he'd any sense he would have run from her. His life had had some sort of order to it before she entered his world. He had wandered the roads of Ireland with various travelling families, and he could count the numbers of fights he'd been involved in on the fingers of one hand, and they had never been serious. Now he had mortally offended another travelling family, and even his own people were reluctant to shelter him because they knew his very presence would probably bring the police around.

Did he love her? He had told her that he didn't, but that wasn't entirely true. Spider had never been short of girl-friends, but he had never come across anyone like Judith Meredith before. He liked her — a lot. He respected her, and cared for her ... was that love? Maybe he simply felt sorry for her because she was so vulnerable and dependent; travellers were used to being dependent on no-one other then them-selves.

Did he hate her? He hated what she had done to him and his lifestyle. He hated the way she had turned his world upside-down, the way she had managed to turn friends into enemies.

Now, here he was in more trouble. He had felt physically sick when he recognised the police car. He had grabbed Judith's hand and pulled her back off the road, and then they had raced through garden after garden, plunging through hedges made brittle by the winter frosts, jumping over low walls, sinking up to their ankles in thawed patches of mud. But it was only now, gasping for breath under the shelter of the bush that he suddenly wondered what the police had thought when they saw him grab the girl and pull her away.

'They'll think I've kidnapped you,' he whispered aloud.

Judith turned to look at him. Strands of blonde hair peeked from under her hood and a twig had scratched her forehead. 'What?'

'The police will think I've kidnapped you,' he repeated.

Judith attempted a laugh. 'Don't be stupid. Why would they think that? Kathleen and her brothers were chasing us, remember.'

'But the police didn't see Mickser running after us, other-wise they would have hauled them in.' He shook his head. 'You've got to go back; you've got to tell the police what happened.'

But Judith shook her head. 'I'm not going back there. Kathleen and her brothers are around, remember?'

'Go and stay with Peggy.'

Judith shook her head. 'I'm staying with you.'

'You can't,' Spider snapped. 'The police will be looking for the two of us.'

Judith put her hand on his arm and squeezed tightly. 'Look, all we have to do is to stay out of trouble until my father and stepmother arrive home tomorrow night. We'll go to my father — both of us — and he'll help us. We'll tell him about Kathleen and what she did and threatened to do. He'll believe me. He'll sort things out with the police.'

Spider shook his head doubtfully, but Judith grabbed his chin and turned his head slightly, forcing him to stare into her eyes. 'Trust me. Anyway,' she added, 'he'll help us simply because he won't want to see me in any more trouble with the police.'

'Judith ...' Spider tried again.

'I'm staying with you, whether you like it or not!' she snapped. 'I got you into this mess; let me try and get you out of it.'

Spider held up both hands in surrender. 'All right, all right, I believe you. Look, we can't stay here. If I'm right, the police will be swarming all over the place shortly. We'll get the DART into town. I know a couple of places we can lie low in.' He paused and added, 'It's going to be uncomfortable, you know that?'

'I know that.'

'You didn't bring money with you by any chance...?'

Judith dug into the pockets of her jeans and came up with two pound coins. Spider added a fifty and twenty pence to the total. 'It'll have to do,' he muttered, knowing that more than half of it would go on the DART fare.

~

They decided to separate going into the DART station. If the police were looking for a couple, they might not look too closely at a young man and woman who arrived at the station five minutes apart and then stood at either end of the platform. When the DART arrived, however, they both got into the same carriage. The train was surprisingly full, mostly with young men and boys, and Judith guessed that there must have been a soccer or rugby match in Bray. She found a seat in the corner by the window, while Spider remained standing. She kept stealing glances at him, comparing him to the other young men standing around him. His features were certainly stronger, and there was more character in his face. While some of the others in the carriage stared numbly through the dirty windows, their eyes dead and unseeing, she noticed that Spider's eyes were constantly moving, roving over the passengers, watching them. Their eyes would meet occasionally but while she smiled — she couldn't help it — his face would remain expressionless.

As the DART pulled into Dun Laoghaire station, Judith realised that the young man sitting opposite was staring at her with a fixed expression, his lips curled in a half smile. When he realised she was looking at him, his smile broadened. Judith bit the inside of her cheek, so as not to show any reaction, and turned away. She suddenly realised that when she'd been smiling at Spider, this guy must have thought she was smiling at him.

She risked a quick glance: short, neatly combed hair, the wisp of a moustache on his upper lip, small indentations on either side of his nose, showing that he wore glasses — she guessed they'd be heavy and ugly — and his teeth were slightly crooked and yellow.

He saw her looking at him and his smile widened.

Judith sighed audibly and deliberately turned away. It was a trick she often used; most boys got the hint. But not this guy. Puzzled by the young woman's reactions — after all she had been smiling pleasantly at him — he glanced around, and immediately discovered that a guy in a battered black leather jacket was staring at her. That's whom she had turned away from!

The train began to empty as they neared the city centre. At Sandymount the seat beside Judith became vacant, and the young man suddenly shifted position to sit beside her. 'Hi,' he muttered.

Judith ignored him.

'Don't worry. I won't let him bother you,' he continued.

Judith turned to look at the young man. 'What?' she said in surprise.

His smile broadened, realising he had her attention. Nodding at Spider, he lowered his voice and whispered conspiratorially. 'Don't worry about him. His type are all show.' He shook his head slightly. 'I don't understand this fashion for men to wear their hair in ponytails. It's so ... effeminate.' He nodded self-importantly. 'I'm Kevin by the way.'

Judith continued to stare at him. She knew if she spoke she would only burst out laughing. She turned back to the window, staring at her reflection in the glass. She saw Kevin frown, then glance up at Spider who was now staring openly at both of them.

Judith turned back to look up at Spider, her eyes wide open, eyebrows raised in an 'I-don't-know' look.

The DART pulled into Pearse St station.

'Where are you getting out?' Kevin asked her.

Spider suddenly stepped up to the seat. 'Why don't you mind your own business,' he hissed.

'Why don't you leave this girl alone?' Kevin demanded loudly.

Spider's smile was vicious. 'I'm not the one who's bothering her.'

'Yes, you are. I've seen you staring at her.'

The raised voices were attracting attention, passengers delighted by the opportunity of a little amusement on the journey. Spider turned away, stooping to glance through the misted-up windows. They were just coming into Tara Street. He glanced at Judith and nodded once. When the train stopped, she immediately stood up and left the train without a backward glance.

Kevin half stood, suddenly beginning to realise that something wasn't right. But then Spider was beside him, his hand on his shoulder, pushing him back into his seat, iron-hard fingers biting deeply in the muscle at the side of his neck. Spider brought his face close to the youth's, saw the sudden fear in his eyes. 'In future, mind your own business,' he hissed. Then he turned and hopped off the train just as the doors closed.

Massaging his bruised shoulder, Kevin watched the couple walk out of the station hand in hand. He was only glad that none of his mates had been around to watch him make a fool of himself.

'I thought you were going to hit him,' Judith said as they stepped out of the station on to the quays. She shivered as an icy wind off the river bit into her face.

'I nearly did. But I didn't want to make a scene,' Spider admitted.

'He was harmless,' Judith said.

'I didn't like his attitude.' Spider grinned. He nodded to the left and they headed down the quays towards O'Connell Street. 'He looked at you and saw a nice girl, and he obviously saw himself as a nice boy. Then he looked at me, and saw something else. He put two and two together and decided that a nice girl like you would want to go with a nice boy like him, and not a gurrier like me.'

'Well, he was wrong, wasn't he?' Judith smiled.

9

The police were waiting at the house when Maxwell and Frankie Meredith arrived home later that night. They were both exhausted and irritable after the flight and the hectic rush from the airport along roads that were already treacherous with ice.

As Maxwell swung the Mercedes into the drive, the headlights picked out two squad cars and an unmarked car parked in front of the house. One of the cars had obviously driven across the grass, leaving deep rutted marks into the soil.

A woman Garda immediately opened the front door, and a long rectangle of warm orange light burst out into the night.

Maxwell stopped the car with a crunch of gravel, climbed out, then walked around to open the door for his wife. As they hurried inside, Maxwell could see his eldest son, Morgan, hovering in the background. He stopped at the door and asked the Garda, 'Any word?'

'Inspector Doyle is waiting inside, sir,' the woman said, giving away no information.

Maxwell caught his son's arm and pulled him to one side. 'What happened?' he demanded.

Morgan shrugged. There were too many years between himself and his younger sister for him to feel really close to her. Right now he resented being called out on a bitterly cold January night because the stupid little girl had vanished. Again. 'I've had a look over the house,' he said. 'The bed in the spare room has been slept in, and someone's used the bathroom. Nothing's been taken,' he added.

'No word from Judith? No note?'

'Nothing.'

Maxwell turned away in disgust and strode into the sitting-room. Inspector Maurice Doyle rose to his feet, his large hand extended. 'I didn't think I'd be seeing you again, sir.'

'Nor I, inspector. Tell me what happened,' he said, shaking the man's hand firmly.

The big man had a notebook in his hand, but he didn't refer to it as he related the simple facts. He ended by saying, 'In my opinion the young man has kidnapped the girl. He was seen dragging her away by the arm.'

'Why couldn't she have gone with him voluntarily?' Frankie asked quietly.

'There is the phone call she made,' the inspector reminded her. 'When our officers arrived, she denied making the call, but I believe the youth was in the house and had probably threatened her.'

Frankie didn't like the inspector's smug attitude. 'But, in the phone call, she said that he was prowling around the garden, while we know for a fact that he spent the night here, sleeping in the spare room. How do you explain that?' she asked innocently.

'Do we?' Puzzled, the inspector looked from Frankie to Maxwell. 'I mean, how do we know the boy spent the night here?'

'The bed in one of the guest rooms has been slept in,' Maxwell explained patiently.

For the first time the inspector consulted his notes; he knew nothing about this. Finally, he said, 'Do we have any evidence that the person who slept in the bed was in fact the boy?'

'None,' Maxwell said. 'But there's no-one else staying here.'

Frankie leaned forward, her eyes on the inspector's round face. 'Why should Judith say on the phone that there was someone in the garden if, in fact, he was already in the house? Why couldn't she simply have told us the truth?'

Maybe he crept into the house before she arrived ...' the inspector began.

'The security system in this house is more sophisticated than in most banks,' Maxwell snapped.

The inspector gave up with a shrug. 'We'll have the answers to all our questions when we find the boy and your daughter.'

'Will you find her, inspector?' Maxwell asked sharply. 'I don't want this turning into another circus.'

'Some of my men were injured in what you call a "circus", sir,' the inspector reminded Maxwell.

'Perhaps if the situation had been handled a little differently, it wouldn't have ended that way,' Maxwell snapped.

The inspector opened his mouth to reply, then suddenly remembered that this man was a personal friend of the Taoiseach and the Commissioner of Police. He had been photographed with the President only last week. He took a breath, calming himself before he said, 'The situation is a little different this time. We've been after this boy for some months now. We know he's living rough on Dublin's streets, stealing and begging what he can. He has no transport. Obviously, he saw your daughter as an opportunity to make some money. I'd imagine you will have a ransom demand within the next few hours. Agree to everything he wants.'

'Let's try and keep this story quiet, eh?'

'Absolutely, Mister Meredith,' the inspector said, concealing a sigh of relief. He didn't want the press in on this. They would rake up last year's story. The boy Spider had made him look a fool. Inspector Doyle hadn't forgotten that, nor forgiven him. 'I'll have your daughter back within twenty-four hours,' the inspector promised.

10

'Where do we go now?' Judith wondered, teeth chattering. They were standing outside the brightly lit Virgin Megastore on Aston Quay. A bitter sleeting drizzle blew down the river, chilling her to the bone. She shivered.

Spider looked at her. 'Please go back home. Go to Peggy; stay there. You'll be safe there.'

Judith stubbornly shook her head.

Spider spun her round, holding her shoulders. His face was so close that she could feel the heat coming off his skin as he stared into her eyes. 'Judith, listen to me. I've got nowhere to go tonight. Nowhere to stay. It's too late to get a bed in one of the hostels, and we haven't enough money for anything else. So we're going to end up sleeping in a doorway, or an abandoned car or a derelict building. It's cold now, but it's going to get colder.' His fingers tightened. ' I'm used to it, but you're not. You could die. People have died on the streets, frozen to death.'

'You're only saying this to frighten me,' Judith protested.

Spider shook his head, water droplets spinning from his hair. 'I'm telling you how it is. But there's no need for you to be part of it. You've enough money for the fare back to Killiney. Stay with your sister-in-law until your father comes back.'

Judith shook herself free of his grip. 'I'm staying with you; only you can keep me safe,' she said defiantly.

Spider shook his head. 'I can't even keep myself safe,' he muttered.

Judith rubbed her gloved hands together. 'Now, where are we going to spend the night?'

~

'Where would they spend the night?' Kathleen asked, leaning forward between the Toyota's front seats. Jed shook his head. He was concentrating on negotiating the car through the road works on Pearse Street. Rotten windscreen wipers screamed across the window, smearing the glass.

'We've looked everywhere over the past few days,' Mickser said. 'He doesn't stay in the hostels, nor in any of the buildings where down-and-outs usually doss out. It was only by chance that we caught up with him yesterday. Mad Mary had spotted him and passed on the word.'

'But he's got the girl with him this time. He'll have to find someplace warm for her to spend the night,' Kathleen said viciously. She tapped her older brother on the shoulder and pointed to the right and Jed swung the car around into Westmoreland Street. 'Mickser, you've spent some time on the streets. What's the first thing he'd do?'

'Eat!' Mickser said.

His older brother grinned. 'You're always thinking of your stomach.'

Mickser shook his head. 'You need a bit of warm food inside you before you lie down for the night. Otherwise you mightn't get up in the morning.'

'Where's the cheapest place to buy food then,' Kathleen demanded, 'places where they'll serve travellers?'

'Takeaways,' Mickser said simply. 'Not the new ones, but the older fish and chippers ....'

'That's where we'll start then.'

'But there's hundreds,' Mickser said. 'We could be out all night.'

'Well then you'd better start now, hadn't you?' Kathleen said savagely.

~

After buying the DART tickets, they had a pound and ten pence left. Spider bought a single of chips for eighty pence and a plastic mug of tea for the remaining thirty pence in a takeaway on the quays, beyond Capel Street Bridge.

The couple ate the chips as they walked down along the quays. 'Chew each chip,' Spider advised. 'Make it last.' They drank sips of the scalding tea, although there was too much sugar for Judith's liking.

Spider stopped at the corner of Capel Street, looking left and then right across the river, wondering where they were going to spend the night. It had just gone seven o'clock but it was already bitterly cold, and although the icy drizzle had stopped, the sky was now clearing to show the brilliantly bright stars. From experience, Spider knew that it was going to get much colder. If he'd been on his own, he would have curled up in a doorway, or under a car, but he didn't think Judith would survive a night in the open. He could feel her shivering by his side and on impulse he put his arm around her. She huddled closer to him.

'Maybe we could spend the night in a church?' she suggested, her teeth chattering.

Spider shook his head, and then, realising that she probably couldn't see the movement, said, 'Nowadays, even churches are locked up at night. During the day you can always find shelter in them, and the priests in most of them don't mind you sitting at the back.'

'You mean some priests do?' she asked in surprise.

Spider grinned, his teeth flashing whitely in the gloom. 'Some do. If you had a nice clean church in a nice clean parish, would you like an old tramp or a vagrant cluttering it up? If the weather's bad tomorrow though, we could spend some time in the Pro or Whitefriar Street'

'The Pro ...?' Judith asked.

'The Pro-Cathedral in Marlborough Street,' he explained. 'When I ran away the first few times, I used to spend a lot of time in it ....' He stopped and suddenly snapped his fingers. 'I just remembered something,' he said. 'Come on; I used to know a place on the quays, but I not sure if its still there, or still usable.'

Judith snuggled close to Spider as they walked down the quays. She felt the ghost of that feeling she'd first experienced the previous summer — a feeling of freedom, of adventure — but now it was tinged with the realisation of very real danger, not only from Kathleen and her brothers, but also from the elements. She knew she could still return to her old life, her safe life, if she wanted to. But she didn't want to. Not just now. The last time she'd run away, her reasons had been selfish. This time she'd run away to help Spider. He had no safe life to return to: she had destroyed that.

They were passing a row of derelict and boarded up shops when Spider slowed, his head turning from side to side. This section of the quays was deserted. 'Keep watch,' he hissed, and stepped up to a heavy-looking door, criss-crossed with bars of wood, and secured with an enormous padlock. Spider ignored the lock. He touched the bars across the door, smiling when he discovered that they hadn't been hammered into place: they were simply for show. Standing right up against the door, he caught one of the bars of wood and lifted the door upwards, jerking it out of its hinges. Spider turned to Judith and placed a finger across his lips, warning her to say nothing. Trying to move as quickly and as quietly as possible, he wrenched the door outwards.

'Inside,' he hissed.

Judith squeezed through the narrow gap. Spider followed and pulled the door back into position, lifting it up, then carefully lowering the pins on the hinges back into place.

Judith was almost glad she was totally blind in what she assumed was a narrow hallway. The stench was incredible, a mixture of mildew and damp, rot and urine; she didn't want to see what made that smell.

A match rasped and flared, and a small yellow circle of wavering light appeared. Spider pulled open a battered electricity meter box and groped around inside, finally emerging with a stub of a candle, which he managed to light just before the match singed his fingers. He then stooped down and examined the floor, the candle-light warm and yellow before him. There were dozens of footprints on the bare floorboards, but they were all coated in a layer of dust, indicating that no-one had been in the house recently.

'Breathe through your mouth?' Spider advised.

Judith nodded, unwilling to speak. She could feel the stench coating her skin; she could even taste it off her lips and tongue.

Spider went first, holding the candle before him in one hand, clutching Judith's hand in the other. She caught brief glimpses of the narrow hallway. The walls were covered with multicoloured graffiti and the tattered remnants of old posters, and there were fast-food bags and burger boxes, crushed drinks cans and crumpled plastic cider bottles everywhere.

The stairway creaked ominously as they climbed slowly, Spider testing each step before he stood on it. Two steps from the top the wood gave way beneath his feet and snapped with the sound of a revolver shot. Judith distinctly heard high-pitched squeaking beneath the broken stair and the sudden rustle of feet. Rats. She imagined a nest of blind and squirming rats beneath the stairs and immediately felt her chips and tea churn in her stomach. Spider hauled her over the broken step on to the landing.

Now that her eyes had adjusted to the gloom, she began to make out some detail. Against the dark walls, six lighter rectangles showed the position of doors. Spider stepped into the nearest doorway, and immediately backed out again, coughing with the appalling stench.

'Smells like a toilet,' Judith whispered, pressing her hand across her mouth.

'Exactly,' Spider muttered. He led her to the room at the end of the hall. The room faced out onto the quays and the street-lamps shed a faint light through windows thickly coated with grime. It was completely bare except for a battered filing cabinet standing against one wall. Three of the drawers hung open; the fourth was missing. There was a small fireplace facing the windows. The mantelpiece and wall above it was smoke and fire-stained.

'This will do,' Spider said, looking around.

Judith said nothing.

'It's either this or spend the night on the streets,' he continued, glancing quickly at her. 'At least we'll be warm here.' Shielding the candle light with his right hand, he walked over to the fireplace and squatted down. Judith followed him. The fireplace was overflowing with burnt scraps of paper and pieces of wood. 'I don't think we'll risk a fire,' he murmured.

'You'd probably burn the place down,' Judith said, attempting a smile.

'We nearly did that on a couple of occasions,' he said rising to his feet.

'You've used this place before,' she asked.

Spider crossed to the window and sat down beneath it, facing the door. Judith squatted beside him on her heels, unwilling to sit on the filthy floor. He lifted the candle. 'I'm putting this out.' Before she could protest, he pinched the wick between forefinger and thumb, plunging the room into darkness.

Judith edged closer to Spider. 'How do you know this place?' she asked.

Spider rested his head against the wall and closed his eyes. 'I think I came here the second time I ran away from home ... that would be five, six years ago. I was about twelve then. Anyway, I'd met up with a guy named Stan, who was a couple of years older than me, a small weedy guy, always in trouble and fights. He'd beg on the Ha'penny Bridge for money, but some of the other beggars would come along and steal it from him, so I used to act as a bodyguard. I was always tough,' he added. Judith's thighs and calves were beginning to ache from squatting, so she sat on the filthy floor and stretched her feet straight out in front of her.

'Draw your knees up to your chest,' Spider advised. 'You'll stay warmer that way.'

She pulled her legs in and snuggled closer to Spider. He hesitated for a moment, then put his arm around her shoulder, drawing her close. Closing her eyes, she tried to ignore the smell and imagine that they were somewhere else, somewhere nice. 'You were telling me about this place,' she reminded him. She felt his head move as he nodded.

'Yes. Stan took me to this place. A lot or runaways used it then. The rooms would be full of mattresses, newspapers and cardboard boxes. Some nights there would be fifteen or twenty people here.'

'What happened?'

The young man shrugged. 'The junkies moved in and turned the place into a shooting gallery.'

Judith turned her head, her hair brushing his cheek. 'A shooting gallery?'

Spider's voice turned hard and bitter. 'Drugs were appearing on Dublin's streets then. Tablets mostly, uppers and downers, and there was a lot of glue sniffing, but there were harder drugs too, like heroin and cocaine. A lot of the street kids are junkies; not all mind you,' he added hastily, 'but a lot. Some are junkies before they come on the street, others are turned into junkies by the street.'

'But not you, Spider,' Judith whispered.

'Not me,' he murmured. 'But it would have been so easy ...' his voice trailed off into a whisper, and she guessed that the memories were painful. 'You see, I was a little different to most kids on the street then. I had a home to go back to. That was my safety net. If things got too tough, I could walk away ....'

'Just like me,' Judith said, but Spider wasn't listening. His eyes were closed and he was seeing this room as it had been six years ago, filled with people, mostly young men, but some young women too, laughing, talking, crying, shouting. He wondered where they were today; he wondered how many of them were still alive.

'I could walk away,' he repeated, 'but so many of them couldn't. They'd ended up on the streets for all sorts of reasons. They weren't stupid though; most of them knew there was no future for them. They knew they would end up begging or stealing. The chances of getting a job without an address were nil. Drugs were the easy way out. A couple of hours of dreams; tablets to give you a high, to make you feel good, glue to give you a buzz, and then eventually on to cocaine and heroin. I know a couple of people who went straight on to heroin. A couple of hours of dreams — and maybe the occasional nightmare. A few hours of escape.'

Judith listened in horrified silence. This was the world she read about in the newspapers, the sort of things she saw on television. But it was always so distant, so abstract. It always happened abroad, never here.

'Stan was a user,' Spider continued very quietly now, almost as if he were speaking to himself. 'He turned other street kids on to drugs in order to support his own habit.' His arm rose, hand closed into a tight fist, finger pointing at the far wall. 'I remember coming in here one night and finding six guys and one girl sitting against that wall shooting up. They had two needles between them. They didn't know about AIDS then ... but I don't think it would have made any difference.'

Judith turned to look at the wall, trying unsuccessfully to visualise the scene. Spider was silent for so long that she finally asked, 'What happened to Stan?'

'It's not the pure drug they stick into their veins,' Spider said quietly. 'The pure stuff would kill them. Sometimes it's diluted — they call it "cut" — with baking soda, sugar or even talcum powder. But sometimes other white powders are used, chalk, brick dust, soap powder, scouring powder.'

Judith shuddered.

'Stan was found dead in the next room. It was reported in the newspaper that his junk had been cut with weed killer.' He paused, then continued quickly. 'I tried to stop him so many times. I fought with him again and again over the drugs. But he couldn't give them up. He had no reason to give them up.' Spider's grip tightened on Judith's shoulder until it became almost painful, then it abruptly relaxed. 'We had a huge argument the night he died. We fought. I discovered his stash of heroin and tossed it on to the fire.' He turned to look at the empty grate. 'I watched him scrabbling amongst the flames, burning his fingers, picking out the little foil packets. He was crying with the pain, but the drugs still meant more to him. I left him then. I never saw him alive again.' There was a long silence, then Spider shifted on the floor. 'Go to sleep,' he said simply.

'It wasn't your fault,' Judith whispered.

Spider didn't reply.

Monday 18th January

11

Kathleen glanced at her cheap digital watch. Half-past midnight. 'Where have they gone?' she raged, pounding the back of the seat with her fist.

Mickser slumped in the front seat, barely able to keep his eyes open. He'd had visited practically every takeaway in the city centre, concentrating on those which gave good value and who had no problems serving travellers. He knew a lot of the staff from the time he had spent on the streets, but no-one had spotted Spider. It was only as they were driving out of the city that he remembered the fish-and-chipper on the quays beyond the Ormond Hotel. While Kathleen and Jed sat in the car, Mickser hurried across Capel Street Bridge, hands dug deep into his pockets, head down against the icy wind that was blowing up the river.

He was in the restaurant less than five minutes and they could tell the moment he came out that he had been successful. He was breathless by the time he reached the car, his cheeks bright red. 'They were there around half-seven, eight, something like that. The girl at the counter saw the spider tattoo.'

'Well, there's nothing more we can do tonight,' Jed muttered, starting the car. 'He's probably found himself a bed for the night. We'll never find him.' He drove down along the deserted quays, heading back for the camp.

'Where are they?' Kathleen fumed.

'Wherever they are,' Jed suddenly grinned, 'I'll bet they're cold and miserable.'

Beside him, Mickser closed his eyes and immediately started to snore.

~

Half-asleep, Frankie rolled over in the bed ... and discovered that Maxwell was missing. She sat up, rubbing the heels of her palms against her eyes, and glanced at the digital display on the bedside clock. 2:44 am. She rolled out of bed and slid her feet into butter-soft suede slippers while pulling on a dressing gown.

Frankie found Maxwell in the kitchen, a cold cup of tea on the table beside him. He was standing with his hands in the pockets of his dressing gown staring out into the black night. He didn't turn as she approached, and when she looked at his face, she was horrified to discover that his eyes were brimming with unshed tears.

'Where is she, Frankie?' he whispered. 'Where has she gone?'

'She'll be back,' his wife soothed him.

'But it's freezing out there,' Maxwell whispered, 'she'll never survive a night on the streets.'

Frankie took his arm and manoeuvred him away from the window. 'She's with Spider,' she said, picking her words with care.

'Who?'

'Spider,' Frankie said slowly.

'What?'

'Spider. That's his name.'

Maxwell sighed. 'Spider. My daughter has disappeared with a boy named Spider. Probably a junkie or a drunk.

God alone knows what he is teaching her, where he's taking her ....'

'Stop that!' Frankie snapped. 'Spider took care of her last year. Maybe if you had taken the time to talk to her about what happened the week she ran away, you would understand her a little better ... you might even understand more about the boy!'

Maxwell bit back an angry reply.

'She did a lot of growing up last year. Most of it thanks to Spider. She told me a lot about him. He kept her out of trouble, protected her, looked after her like a big brother.' Frankie squeezed his arm tightly. 'You need have no worries about Spider. He doesn't drink and he is not a drug user. He's not going to hurt her. Just be thankful that he's looking after her.'

~

In the derelict building on the quays, Judith and Spider slept side by side, warmed by each other's body heat.

12

In her dream she couldn't move, couldn't breathe.

Judith Meredith's eyes widened with shock as she came fully awake and realised that she really couldn't move, and that she had to fight to draw every breath into her lungs.

She had fallen asleep sitting on the floor, with her knees drawn up to her chest, her arms wrapped around her shins, her head on her knees. Her last conscious thoughts had been of the comforting weight of Spider's arm across her shoulders.

Spider! Where was Spider?

With an enormous effort of will, Judith managed to raise her head off her knees. Taut muscles along her neck and back protested and her spine felt like a rigid iron bar. Pressing her back against the cold wall, she straightened out her legs, muscles cracking, knees popping. Pins and needles bit into her toes, curled her fingers. Shaking her hands to restore circulation, she was forced to wait until feeling returned to her toes, then she came unsteadily to her feet, her hand pressed to the small of her back. Her bottom was numb.

Where was Spider?

She glanced at her watch. The glowing hands showed seven o'clock. It was still dark outside. Maybe he'd left her in the middle of the night. Even though the thought was terrifying, she knew it made sense. He knew she wasn't going to leave him alone, so all she was doing was slowing him down. Why shouldn't he leave her?

As she staggered out on to the landing, she heard a noise from below, the creaking sound of the door being opened. She was about to call "Spider", but stopped herself. What if it wasn't Spider? What if it was one of the other street people who used this derelict building? And what were they going to say when they discovered her?

What would they do?

A match rasped below and then a flickering light danced across the mildewed walls. Footsteps sounded on the stairs and she backed into the room. The candle-light threw a long distorted shadow up the wall ... and a shape stepped on to the landing. It turned towards her and lifted the candle ... and suddenly she was running forward, throwing her arms around Spider, realising just how terrified she had been.

'I woke up and I didn't know and I thought and then I heard ....' It all came out in a rush.

'I went out to get breakfast,' he said gently, manoeuvring her back into the room.

'We have no money,' Judith began, but then she saw the two cartons of milk and the loaf of bread nestled in the crook of Spider's arm. 'How?'

'If I tell you, you'll get upset and probably refuse to eat.'

'I'm hungry. I'll eat. Now tell me where you got the milk and bread.'

Spider squatted down on the floor, shook the two cartons of milk, then tore a triangular strip off the top of each. He passed one up to the girl. 'Every morning milk and bread, washed vegetables and bags of chips are delivered to restaurants all across the city. If no-one's there to take them in, they're left outside.' He grinned. 'I wasn't sure what we could do with a large bag of washed and cut potatoes.'

Judith looked at the milk and bread. 'You stole it.'

'Borrowed it,' he said easily. 'Right now, we have no money.' His smile faded when he saw that Judith didn't touch the milk. 'I thought you said you were hungry?'

'I was ... I am.'

'Then you have a choice: eat or starve,' he said bluntly. He tilted back his head and drank deeply from the carton of milk. He rubbed his sleeve across his mouth, wiping away a white milk moustache. 'Listen to me, Judith. When you've lived on the streets as long as I have, you learn not to be so choosy. When you're hungry, you'll take whatever food you can. Stealing from restaurants in the morning is easy. At least the food is clean and fresh. But after a while, you'll start rooting in bins; you'll get to know which restaurants throw out food, you'll discover where the supermarket bins are kept. You'll start begging for money for plastic cups of tea; you'll eat crisps, lots of crisps, because they're cheap and they fill you up. Maybe if you manage to beg enough you'll buy a Mars bar; you can go for a whole day on a Mars bar.' Spider stopped, ashamed of his outburst. 'I'm sorry,' he said. 'But you'll find that when you're living on the streets, you can't afford to have too many scruples.' He lifted the milk carton, and Judith drank.

They sat in silence, drinking the cold milk, eating slices of dry bread, while outside the traffic on the quays gradually increased, car tyres humming on the concrete, horns honking and once they heard a distant crash as two cars collided on the icy road. A few moments later an ambulance fought its way through the early morning traffic. The room slowly brightened as grey light filtered through the filthy windows. In daylight it looked even more squalid and Judith discovered to her horror that the floor was coated in a layer of black grease. Her 501s and expensive waxed coat were smeared with the grime. She lifted her hands to her face: they too were filthy.

'There's no water,' Spider said, before she could ask. 'Nor is there a toilet,' he said, anticipating her next question. He smiled humourlessly. 'However, you've got this whole house to yourself. Pick a room.'

Judith swallowed hard. 'What about a public toilet? There must be one close by.'

'Have you any money?'

She shook her head. 'What about an hotel, or a pub ....'

Spider leaned over and gently touched her face, brushing strands of hair from her cheek. 'You look like a traveller; you smell like a traveller,' he added, smiling, to take the sting from the words. 'A lot of pubs won't let you past the door.'

'How can you live like this?' Judith demanded, voice quivering with frustration and rage.

'Not through choice,' Spider said coldly. 'I don't like this any more than you do. But I haven't got a choice. I've no home to go back to.' He stopped, regretting his words the moment they were spoken.

Judith took a deep breath before replying. She knew what he was saying was true. It wasn't his fault that he was living in this squalor. It was hers.

'I've been thinking about that,' she said slowly. She drank some more of the milk, but she was reluctant to touch the bread with her filthy fingers. 'You've got two problems — besides me,' she added with a wan smile.

'Only two?' he wondered, picking at a slice of bread, rolling it into a ball.

'The police are looking for you because of what happened last year. Let's leave that to one side for a moment; I'm sure my father could sort that out. But the police also think you're committing these burglaries.'

Spider nodded. 'Apparently it's someone with a traveller accent — naturally they think it's me.'

'If we could find out who's committing the burglaries, that would sort out that problem.'

Spider laughed briefly. 'I wish it was that simple.'

'Then there's Kathleen and her brothers. What would satisfy them? Money?'

He nodded. 'Money and a new van.'

'My father can sort that out too,' Judith said firmly.

'Just like that?' he asked, unable to keep the sarcasm from his voice.

Judith nodded. 'Just like that.'

'Its not that simple, Judith,' Spider said gently. 'You're assuming that your father will want to help.'

'He will,' she said confidently.

'Why?'

Judith looked at Spider in astonishment. 'Because he's never refused me anything in my life.'

The young man shrugged. He couldn't argue with that. Although he and Judith both lived in Dublin, they occupied very different worlds, with different values and morals.

'So, let's concentrate on this burglar.'

'Burglars,' Spider corrected her, holding up two fingers. 'There are at least two; one drives a van.'

'Have you never tried to find out who they are?'

Spider shook his head. 'I never had a reason to find out. I was too busy staying out of trouble.' He finished off the milk as he considered her question. If he really wanted to know, who would he ask?

'You could find out, couldn't you?' Judith whispered, watching his expression. She was learning to read his face. Now she saw his eyes glazing over, his lips tightening, lines gathering around his eyes and mouth.

'I could ask around. It's risky though ...' he began.

'I'm coming with you,' she said, before he could object.

Spider sighed. 'I didn't think I'd any choice.' Judith suddenly hopped to her feet. 'Where are you going?' he asked.

'To the toilet,' she muttered, hurrying from the room.

~

In a line of traffic directly opposite the derelict building, Kathleen with her father and two brothers sat in the battered Toyota. No-one was speaking. There had been a blazing argument earlier when Kathleen woke everyone at six-thirty, to get them up to renew the hunt for Spider and Judith.

'You're becoming obsessed,' Jed muttered over breakfast.

'Maybe I am,' she hissed, 'but I want you to teach him a lesson. Break his legs.'

Her brothers glanced sidelong at their father on the other side of the table, but he kept his head down and added salt to his porridge.

'I want the girl taught a lesson too,' Kathleen added.

But Mickser shook his head. 'Leave the girl out of this. I'm not beating up on no girl.'

'I'm not asking you to. Just bring her to me. I'll take care of it.'

'Today!' Joe Ryan exclaimed. 'If you don't get them today, forget about it. We've got other business.'

'Da ...' Kathleen began, but her father slapped his hand down on the table, making everything shudder and rattle.

'Today! If you catch the boy, teach him a lesson. He stole from us, dishonoured us. But leave the girl alone. She's not one of us. You hurt her and she'll bring the coppers in. And we don't want that, do we?'

One by one they shook their heads.

~

Maxwell Meredith allowed his breakfast to grow cold. He turned the pages of *The Irish Times*, but was unable to concentrate on it. Finally he flung it down and looked at Frankie, sitting across from him.

'I've got to do something.'

'The police are doing all they can,' his wife said slowly.

'The police couldn't catch them last year, and even when they had them, they couldn't hold the boy. If he'd been locked up, none of this would have happened.'

Frankie drank her tea, realising that her husband wasn't looking for advice, he simply needed someone to talk to.

'There's a firm of private detectives the company uses occasionally. I was thinking of bringing them in, getting them to look for Judith and the boy.'

13

Getting out of the derelict house proved far more difficult than getting in. Although traffic thinned out considerably after nine thirty, there was still a fairly steady stream of cars along the quays, and the occasional pedestrian passed by the boarded-up door.

Judith stood behind Spider in the hallway. He was peering through a crack in the door, patiently biding his time, though Judith was becoming more and more frustrated with the delay.

'We could be here all day at this rate,' she muttered.

'You're right,' he agreed. 'But we can't just step out of a derelict building. Someone would be sure to notice and maybe report it to the police. I'm waiting until traffic is moving fairly freely. Then, even if someone does see us, they'll have driven past before they realise what they were looking at. But I don't want to step out when someone's passing by.'

Several minutes passed, then he suddenly said, 'Get ready. As soon as I lift the door, slip out, then walk away immediately. Go down the quays towards the Ha'penny Bridge. I'll catch up with you later. Don't linger, and don't look back.

Ready ....' He re-adjusted his grip on the door and wrenched it upwards. 'Now go!'

Judith slipped through the narrow opening and stepped out on to the pavement. Digging her hands deep into her pockets, she turned and walked down the quays. Her shoulders were rigid with tension: she expected a car to stop or someone to run up and grab her shoulder.

She slowed when she came to the small art gallery just beside the Woollen Mills facing the Ha'penny Bridge. Pretending to look at the oil and water-colour paintings, she waited for Spider. She glanced up, looking into the darkened shop — and saw her own reflection — and was shocked by what she saw. A night of sleeping in the derelict house had left deep shadows beneath her red-rimmed eyes, which seemed to have sunk into her head. Her skin was unnaturally pale, and the dark smudges of dirt stood out clearly. Several strands of her blond hair, now dark and greasy, curled down on to her forehead. Her clothes were soiled; she felt dirty and she smelled of damp and mildew. She desperately wanted to brush her teeth which felt coated with fur.

Spider appeared by her side. Looking at him critically, she realised that he didn't look as dirty and dishevelled as she did, nor did he look as tired. Maybe it was possible to get used to this way of life, but she knew she never would.

'Any problems?' she asked.

The young man shook his head and grinned. 'So long as you act as if you've every right to be doing what you're doing, people will not look twice at you. Once you start acting suspiciously, they'll watch your every move.'

'Where are we going now?' Judith asked, as they turned left into Liffey Street.

'We're going to meet Tyrrell. If anyone knows who's doing the burglaries, he will.'

'Why?' Judith wondered.

Spider smiled wolfishly. 'Because he's a fence: he deals in stolen goods.'

~

Barbara Harper sat opposite Maxwell and Frankie, listening carefully to their story, making notes in a small leather note-book. She questioned them both about the last time Judith had run away, and listened carefully when Frankie spoke about Judith's reaction to Spider. Finally she requested a recent photograph of the girl.

'I'll need to keep this,' she said, sliding the colour photo-graph out of the frame. It showed Judith sitting on a long wooden bench surrounded by brilliantly coloured rose bushes.

Maxwell nodded. 'Of course. Take whatever you need.' He had used Harper Investigations on several occasions in the past. They were very successful, extremely discrete, and very expensive. 'Send the bill to me,' Maxwell continued. 'This is not to go on the corporate account.'

'Of course,' Barbara Harper said and made a note. She was a small stout woman in her late forties, with an oval face and fashionably short, dyed black hair. She looked like anything but a private detective.

'You will handle the case discreetly?' Maxwell asked. 'I don't want any more publicity after the affair last year.'

'I will be working on this case personally, and I guarantee that nothing will leak from our end.' She spoke with a soft Dublin accent. 'We will look into this boy Spider's back-ground, access his police record, look for known associates, check up on his regular haunts. I believe the route to your daughter lies through the boy.' She stood up and slipped her notebook and the photograph into a slim leather suitcase. As Frankie and Maxwell led her to the door, he asked, 'What makes a girl like Judith run away with a boy like this?'

Barbara Harper turned to look at him, eyes wide with surprise. 'Why, love of course, Mister Maxwell. Love.'

~

Judith had been in the ILAC Centre two days previously. She'd spent nearly two hours wandering around, looking in windows, trying on jeans and leather jackets — she wanted a studded leather jacket — boots and shoes. The place had been bright and airy, full of people, the air buzzing with hundreds of voices. Even though it was January, she'd had an ice cream and eaten it sitting by the pool, watching the people swarm around, listening to the buzz of conversation. She'd felt relaxed and at ease.

Now she saw how the security men looked at her and Spider as they pushed their way through the Henry Street entrance, just beside Easons. She saw one man raise his walkie-talkie to his mouth and she knew instinctively that he was talking about her. As she and Spider rounded the corner by the lifts she saw another security man turn to look at them.

Judith discovered that she was acutely aware of the smell of fresh bread and coffee from the patisserie and restaurants, and she felt her stomach grumble.

Spider squeezed her shoulder. 'Don't worry. I'll find us something to eat soon. Real food too,' he promised.

She attempted a smile, which failed.

'What time is it?' Spider asked as they approached the pool in the centre of the ILAC.

Judith glanced at her watch. 'Just after ten. Why?'

He nodded to the stairs on the left. 'The library is up there. Later on in the day, usually around lunchtime, there'll be a crowd in there, and you can go in and sit down. You can watch videos and listen to music.' He glanced sidelong at Judith. 'I'm practising my reading.'

Judith looked up the stairs. 'Why can't we go in now?'

'Because, it's only been open a few minutes. We'd probably be the only ones in there, and we'd stick out like sore thumbs. We can come back though.'

They left the ILAC through the Moore Street entrance and turned left, past stalls of fish and vegetables and flowers. Close to the bottom of the street, Spider murmured a quick 'Stay here,' to Judith and crossed the street to one of the stalls. He spoke to the stall-keeper, a tall, thin, sharp-faced woman wearing a long apron over her coat. She lifted her head to glare at Judith before turning back to Spider.

When Spider returned a few moments later, he was carrying a large paper bag, bulging with apples, oranges, bananas and tomatoes.

'You had no money, Spider,' Judith said slowly.

'I didn't pay. Betty would've been insulted if I'd even offered.'

'But why?'

'I did her a favour once; let's leave it at that.'

Judith nodded. She broke a banana off the bunch and peeled it slowly, being careful not to touch the fruit with her dirty fingers.

They walked on in silence, turned right at the bottom of the street, then left into Parnell Square. They continued up past the Wax Museum and turned right into Dorset Street.

'Now whatever happens here,' Spider said suddenly, speaking for the first time since they had left Moore Street, 'whatever happens, you say nothing, you do nothing. Understand?'

Judith nodded. 'You make it sound as if this is dangerous.'

'It could be,' he said quietly. 'We're going to see Tyrrell. He's called Tyrrell the Squirrel, but never to his face. He buys and sells stolen goods. He finances robberies, supplying the money and material necessary to do the job — in return for a handsome cut, of course.'

'How do you know him?'

'When Stan needed money for drugs, he would steal. He'd break into cars, snatch handbags, smash and grab from shops. I discovered that he was selling the stuff to Tyrrell, who'd give him something like one tenth of the value of the goods. When Stan died, I went to Tyrrell, told him what had happened, the damage the money he'd given Stan had caused. I think I even accused him of murdering Stan.'

'What did he do?'

'He laughed. Told me it was business. Simply business. Then he asked me if there was anything I wanted to sell him.'

Spider turned into a narrow side-street off Dorset Street, lined with two rows of neat cottages. He stopped half way down the street, before a house that looked identical to all the others. The garden was neatly tended with a pair of ridiculous gnomes in the centre of a bedraggled flower bed. Judith saw curtains twitching as they walked up the path.

Spider paused before pressing the bell and glanced at Judith. 'Say nothing.' His forefinger hadn't quite touched the bell when the door opened silently inwards.

Gripping Judith's hand tightly, Spider stepped into the gloom. The door clicked shut behind them, an electronic lock clicking into place.

Spider turned to the left at the bottom of the narrow hallway into the sittingroom. Judith's first impression was of clutter, of overlarge expensive furniture that was out of place in the small room. An enormous television set took up most of the nook beside the fire. In the opposite nook, a sleek black stereo system sat on top of a glass-fronted cabinet.

A high-backed studded leather chair was positioned beside the coal fire and as the couple entered the room, a slender hand appeared above the chair, pointing to the settee. Judith looked at Spider who merely shrugged and sat down.

Moments later the door opened and a short squat young man entered. His hair was shaved close to his skull, and a carefully cultivated moustache drooped over his top lip. He was wearing black and white army trousers tucked into eighteen hole Doc Martens and a black tee-shirt which showed off the muscles of his chest and arms. Ignoring the couple, he perched on the windowledge, folded his arms and watched the television. A BBC school's programme was just coming to a close.

The leather chair swung round suddenly. 'Spider. It's been a long time.'

'Mr Tyrrell,' Spider said carefully.

Judith had been expecting someone seedy, but Tyrrell was the exact opposite. The man was in his mid-forties, small, neat, distinguished-looking, with snow white hair and startlingly black eyebrows. His face was smooth and unlined and his bright blue eyes were slightly magnified behind gold-rimmed glasses. He was wearing grey slacks, a grey shirt open at the neck, rust-coloured slippers and a bright yellow jumper with a small green crocodile on the breast. He looked like a priest or a schoolteacher, Judith decided.

'What can I do for you, Spider?' Tyrrell asked pleasantly, his eyes darting from the young man to the young woman. They kept lingering on the girl.

'I need your help, Mr Tyrrell,' Spider said evenly.

Tyrrell's smiled broadened, revealing perfectly white teeth. 'I always said you'd come back, Spider. I'm surprised it's taken so long. What can I do for you?'

'I need some information, Mr Tyrrell.'

The older man's smiled faded. 'I don't deal in information.'

Spider leaned forward, watching the fence carefully. He wasn't fooled by Tyrrell's pleasant exterior. The man hadn't become successful in his particular business by being nice to people. 'I'm looking for information about some people you might have had dealings with.'

Tyrrell's smile vanished completely, and the young man by the window straightened, his arms falling to his side, sensing trouble.

Spider continued staring at Tyrrell. 'You know the police are looking for me?'

'I've heard something to that effect.'

'They believe I've carried out a series of robberies and break-ins. All I know is that the police think it's a traveller. I think you might know more,' he smiled.

Tyrrell started to shake his head. 'I don't know what you're talking about. And even if I did, why should I tell you anything?'

Spider's smile turned into a savage grin. 'Because when the police catch me — as they surely will — I might just tell them all I know about you.'

The older man shook his head. 'If I had a penny for every time I've heard that threat ....'

'It's not a threat,' the young traveller said icily. 'Stan told me a lot about you. You remember Stan, don't you?'

'Tommy,' Tyrrell said, without turning his head, 'show Spider and his friend to the door. And convince him that it would be unhealthy to talk about me.'

The youth moved away from the window and reached for Spider. 'Let's go,' he grinned. And then his grin vanished as Spider lashed out with his booted foot, catching the youth in the groin, dropping him to the floor, his face ashen. His scream turned into a high-pitched whistle. Spider caught Tommy's arm as he fell and twisted it savagely, forcing the youth downwards, his face in the deep-pile carpet. It had happened in seconds ... and Spider had remained seated.

Tyrrell attempted a smile. 'It seems you deserve your reputation.'

'Will you tell me what I want to know?' Spider demanded.

Tyrrell shook his head.

'I'll break his arm.' Spider twisted the youth's hand and wrist, making him grunt in pain.

Tyrrell shrugged. 'Do it. That's what he gets paid for. When you're gone, I'll send him down to the Mater Hospital and pay him a bonus.'

Judith was appalled by the callousness in the man's voice. 'Will you sell us the information, Mr Tyrrell?' she asked suddenly.

The fence shifted his attention to the young woman. He'd realised the moment she walked into the room that there was something strange about her. And her accent definitely wasn't that of a traveller. 'I might be prepared to do a deal,' he said quietly. 'What have you go to sell?' he asked. He wanted to hear her speak again.

Judith reached inside the collar of her coat with both hands, fiddled around the back of her neck and held out a fine wire necklace which was made of plaited strands of white, red and yellow gold.

Tyrrell caught the girl's dirty hand, feeling its softness, seeing her perfectly manicured nails before taking the necklace from the palm of her hand. He felt its weight and expertly gauged its value at around fifteen hundred pounds.

'Do you want to sell this?'

'I'll trade it for the names of the thieves.'

Tyrrell nodded. 'It's Kathleen Ryan and her brothers, Jed and Mickser. Joe, the father, drives the van.' His hand closed into a fist, clutching the necklace tightly. 'As a bonus, I'll tell you that they're due to hit a warehouse on the quays tonight,' he continued. He scribbled an address on the back of an envelope and passed it across. 'Don't tell them I sent you,' he added with a smile.

'No honour amongst thieves, eh?' Spider asked.

Tyrrell shrugged. 'Just business.'

14

Judith and Spider sat on the long benches in the Garden of Remembrance and ate the remainder of the fruit. The January sunshine gave no warmth, however, and they were both chilled through. Judith desperately needed a cup of hot tea.

They had barely spoken since leaving Tyrrell's. Spider had been eager to put as much distance as possible between themselves and the fence, just in case he sent his muscle-bound bodyguard after them. Judith had to trot to keep up with his long-legged stride.

When she realised that they were opposite the Garden of Remembrance, she grabbed his arm and pulled him to a halt. 'I'm out of breath,' she panted. 'There's no-one following us. I need to sit down.' There was a break in the traffic and she hauled Spider across the road and through the iron gates. The garden was deserted. Spider chose seats below the level of the gates, facing into the sunshine, allowing them some shelter from the cutting breeze. They were also hidden from any passers-by.

Spider finished the last of the apples and was about to throw the butt into the ornamental pool when he saw the look on

Judith's face and sheepishly dropped it into the paper bag. He rubbed his hands on his jacket and turned in the seat to look at the young woman.

'You didn't have to give Tyrrell your necklace.'

'He gave us the information we needed.'

'He would have given it anyway,' Spider said grimly.

'Violence isn't the only way,' she said fiercely. 'And I didn't want to see you get hurt,' she added.

Spider suddenly leaned forward and kissed her on the cheek. His hand found hers and he squeezed her fingers gently. 'When this is all over, I'll get your necklace back for you. I promise.'

'The necklace isn't important, Spider. What is important is proving your innocence. I think we should go to the police.'

Spider blinked in surprise.

Judith pressed on. 'We can tell them about Kathleen and her brothers and the robbery tonight ....'

But Spider was shaking his head.

'Why not?' she demanded coldly.

'Judith, think about it. Do you think the police are going to believe us? They're not going to listen to us .... And besides, what proof have we got? The word of a known fence.'

'We've got to do something,' she insisted.

Spider nodded. 'I know that,' he replied. Swivelling around on the wooden seat, he folded his arms across his chest, tucking his hands into his armpits for warmth.

Judith turned sideways to look at him. The expression on his face was frightening; the muscles around his eyes and mouth had tightened into a hard mask; his lips were set in a thin line. At that moment, his face looked very cruel.

Spider caught her looking at him and raised his eyebrows in a silent question.

'I was wondering what you were thinking.'

'I was thinking that we need to be able to prove to the police that Kathleen, Jed and Mickser are responsible for the robberies.' He straightened up, staring hard at the long narrow pool of green water. 'The police need to catch them with the stolen goods on them.'

Judith shook her head. 'I'm not sure what you're getting at.'

Spider turned in the seat. 'Don't you see? If the police were to catch them with the stolen goods, then there would be no doubt of my innocence. And they'd get a prison sentence.'

'Two birds with one stone.'

'Exactly,' Spider muttered. 'We'll need to think about this very carefully.'

Judith shivered, and Spider slid closer on the wooden seat and slipped his arm around her shoulder. 'Don't worry. It'll be all over soon. And I've got you to thank for it.'

'Me?' she asked in surprise.

'If you hadn't encouraged me to face Kathleen, I'd still be running. Now, you've given me the chance.' He turned her chin and looked into her large brown eyes. 'I won't waste it.' He kissed her again, his breath warm and moist on her lips.

~

The sky clouded over in the early afternoon, dark ugly clouds pushed in by an icy wind that spat sleet and the odd whirling flake of snow on to the city. The temperature fell sharply and by four o'clock the streets were beginning to freeze over and the early evening traffic had slowed to a crawl. When it started to snow less than an hour later, huge silent flakes that quickly coated the streets and parked cars, the traffic ground to a complete halt.

Maxwell Meredith sat in his car in a traffic jam in Merrion Square and listened patiently on his car phone while Barbara Harper made her report. Occasionally the signal would fade and her voice would dissolve into an irritating hiss.

'Look, you're not telling me anything I don't know,' Meredith snapped, frustrated by the phone, the appalling traffic and a hectic day at the office. 'I don't want to know where the boy has been or what he has done. I want to know where he is now!'

Barbara Harper sat in her office in Pearse Street, looking down on four solid lines of traffic. Horns blared and lights flashed as motorists vented their frustration, but nothing was moving.

'We've contacted as many of his known associates as possible,' she said calmly, then waited while the line crackled maddeningly. 'At the moment we're trying to catch up with a Miss Kathleen Ryan, and her brothers, Jed and Mickser Ryan. They've been involved with the boy in the past; when Spider was caught last year he was driving their van. They claim he stole it, but it seems unlikely. They probably lent it to him, but when he wrecked it, decided that they'd stand a better chance of compensation if they reported it stolen. We traced the Ryan family to a site on the Navan Road, but they didn't turn up all day. They don't seem to be particularly well liked by the other travellers. I've got someone watching the place now,' she added.

'Do you think Judith and Spider are with them?'

'It's a chance,' Barbara Harper replied. 'The two Ryan boys have been in trouble with the law before. So has the father. So has Spider. Draw your own conclusions.'

'Keep me in touch,' Maxwell Meredith said, turning off the phone and passing it forward to the chauffeur's raised hand.

'No quick way home tonight, sir,' the chauffeur said cheerily. 'I certainly wouldn't like to be out in this.'

Maxwell Meredith turned his face to the window, blinking furiously, determined not to allow the chauffeur to see the tears in his eyes. He looked out at the snow-swept streets and wondered where his daughter was.

~

The Ryans had intended heading back to the caravan before setting off on the job, but the sudden deterioration in the weather changed all that. With traffic reduced to an inching crawl, even considering leaving the city was madness.

They ate in a small café on the quays, just off O'Connell street, sitting at the window, watching the snow falling, turning to filthy slush on the streets and paths, but gathering thickly elsewhere.

'This weather will help us,' Kathleen muttered. She saw Mickser's blank expression and explained, 'No-one, not even security guards, will be out on a night like this.'

He nodded doubtfully. He preferred to leave all the planning to his younger sister.

The Ryans had always been petty thieves, stealing cars and vans, breaking into houses and shops, even robbing horses from other travellers. They weren't always successful and so far, only Kathleen hadn't been caught and served time. The last time Joe had been in prison, Kathleen had started choosing the jobs for her brothers, picking out the shops and houses which were easy pickings. She had two rules: no dogs and no burglar alarms. If she discovered either, then she simply picked another house. She had the patience to sit and watch a property for weeks, learning the routine, until she could tell almost to the minute how long a house would remain empty, or when a shop was restocked.

But recently Kathleen had grown tired of the relatively small pickings, and set her sights on larger shops and warehouses. Once again, she picked the targets and did most of the planning herself. When they were stealing from a shop, they simply loaded up the van with as much stuff as they could carry, but she insisted that when they stole from a warehouse, they were to take only what they could easily sell, and ignore anything unusual or instantly identifiable. Tonight, they were after a cache of the latest flat-screen televisions and videos. There was also a consignment of computers in the warehouse, but she knew they'd have difficulty disposing of the machines and Jed and Mickser had instructions to ignore them. She'd been planning this job for months, and it was going to be their most lucrative yet.

Joe Ryan lit up a cigarette and stuck it in the corner of his mouth. Smoke trickled up into his left eye, making him squint. 'Maybe we should call it off.'

'Why?' Kathleen demanded aggressively.

'Because if this weather keeps up, by eleven o'clock tonight not only will the roads be skating rinks, but there'll be damn-all traffic around. We're going to stick out like a sore thumb.' He grinned, showing the remains of his stained teeth. 'We don't want to be stopped by the police.'

Jed nodded. 'I agree with Da. Why don't we put it off for a night at least?'

'Because,' Kathleen said in a fierce whisper, 'the goods will be moved first thing in the morning. It has to be done tonight.'

'We could have done it last night if you hadn't been wandering around looking for your old boyfriend.'

Kathleen's smile was bitter as she looked out onto the quays. 'I hope he and his girlfriend are enjoying their night on the town.'

~

Spider had predicted that it was going to snow at least an hour before the first flake had fallen from the sky. He had led a cold and miserable Judith Meredith down O'Connell Street. The smells from the fast-food restaurants were mouthwatering, and her stomach was empty. She found herself staring at the people sitting in the windows, eating burgers and chips, drinking tea and coffee and milkshakes. As they walked past Burger King, she watched a girl of around her own age dump half a burger and a handful of chips into a bin. For a brief moment she felt angry — angry at the girl for wasting the food, and angry at herself, because her first instinct had been to run inside and dig into the bin. Her reaction had shaken her; was this all it took to strip away her self-control and dignity?

They turned to the left at Burger King into Cathedral Street, and then climbed up the steps of the Pro-Cathedral. Spider entered by a side door, murmuring that there was usually a traveller begging at the front steps, and that he might be recognised.

It was warm inside the church, the air dry and scented with the waxy scent of burning candles and the old odour of incense. The young man moved confidently around the dark interior, choosing a shadowed seat on the left-hand side of the church close enough to the side door, but which also allowed him to see who entered by the main door. Judith was shocked to discover that they were not the only down-and-outs in the church. An incredibly wizened old man, bundled up in dozens of coats, was stretched out on a seat across from them, while a man and women, not much older than themselves, drank from a bottle in a brown-paper bag, passing it back and forth in silence.

'What do we do now?' Judith whispered.

'Relax,' Spider muttered. 'Try and get some sleep; it's going to be a long night.'

15

Judith dozed off in the church, a combination of silence and warmth, her own exhaustion and lack of food sending her to sleep sitting up on the hard wooden seat. She woke with a start, her heart pounding madly as she looked around, desperately wondering where she was. When she realised she was alone, she experienced sudden terror.

She rose stiffly to her feet ... and immediately sat down again. In the main body of the church, evening mass was in progress. She wanted to leave, and yet if she left, Spider wouldn't know where to find her. All she could do was sit and wait, and hope he returned.

But as the mass progressed and there was no sign of Spider, her apprehension grew. When she turned around to check the doors, she was shocked to discover that there were now a dozen down-and-outs, old and young alike, sitting at the back of the church, bundled up in layers of clothing. The door opened in a gust of cold air and a young woman scurried inside and blessed herself. Her head and shoulders and one side of her coat were thickly crusted with snow.

Judith felt very afraid. Last night had been cold enough, but how were they going to survive a night like this on the streets?

When she turned around again Spider had slid into the seat beside her. He was brushing snow from his hair and jacket. His flesh was the colour of stone, although his nose and cheekbones were red. She placed the back of her hand against his cheek, and winced with its chill. But he was grinning, his eyes like black holes in his pale face. 'Come on,' he whispered.

'We're not going out in that weather,' she murmured.

'I've taken care of it. Come on.' He caught her hand in his and pulled her towards the door. Taking a deep breath, Judith stepped out of the church ... and into a blizzard. The cold bit into her chest, searing the back of her throat. A sudden pain lanced behind her eyes and settled in over the bridge of her nose. She'd experienced a similar pain once before when she'd eaten a cold ice-cream one summer's day. She could see less than half a dozen steps in front of her and her fingers were so numb that she couldn't actually feel Spider's hand in hers.

Spider led her down the steps of the Pro-Cathedral and around into Marlborough Street, which was ghostly beneath a thick covering of snow. The street lights painted the scene an eerie sodium yellow, and she became aware of the silence, the snow dulling all the normal city sounds. They were the only pedestrians and there were no cars moving on the road.

Spider stopped, looked up and down the street, then abruptly pulled open the door of a Volkswagen Beetle and practically pushed Judith inside, slamming the door hard after her. Three inches of packed snow shifted off the car's sloped roof. He wiped the windscreen clear of snow as he scurried around to the driver's side and slid in behind the wheel.

Judith attempted to speak, but her teeth were chattering madly and she couldn't formulate the question. She watched numbly as Spider fiddled beneath the steering wheel, finally wrenching out a bundle of wires. Selecting two, he twisted them together in a flicker of sparks ... and the car coughed into life. He gently eased it out of the parking space, the wheels whirring on the icy ground.

'You've stolen this!' Judith accused.

Spider ignored her and concentrated on driving. The windscreen wipers could barely cope with the snow, and thick ridges were forming at the base of the window. He'd have to get out soon and clean it off.

Judith Meredith was cold and hungry, she'd never felt so tired in her life, and she was dirty. She could smell the odour of her own stale sweat, and she hated it. All her frustrations bubbled up into a cold anger.

'You've stolen this car!'

Spider gave her a sidelong glance at her, wondering if she was joking.

'You're a thief,' she breathed.

Spider frowned. Didn't she realise he'd stolen the car for her benefit, not his? 'I've stolen it — so what?'

'And you've done it before too,' she accused.

Spider applied the brake gently and felt the car shift sideways on the road. 'And how do you make that out?' he demanded.

'You got into this car without any trouble and you hot-wired the engine like an expert.'

'Any street kid in Dublin could do the same,' Spider snapped. 'Remember, Miss Meredith, that's what I am: a Dublin street kid.'

'Just like Kathleen and her brothers?' Judith said quietly, but loud enough for him to hear.

'Just like them,' he agreed.

They drove on in silence. When the engine had warmed up, Spider flicked on the heaters, blasting warm air into the car, both of them glad of the noise filling the bitter silence that hung between them. Spider turned left down the quays, carefully guiding the Beetle into a gentle glide. The VW had a tendency to drift to the left, he noticed. It hadn't exactly been his first choice, and he hadn't taken it because it was any easier to steal; Spider could have taken any of the parked cars on the street. His first inclination was to take something fast and powerful, but it would only be a liability on a night like this. Not only would it stand out on the deserted roads, but its power would make it dangerous. No, he needed something innocent looking. A car that wouldn't raise a second glance from a police officer ... or a suspicious thief.

They were driving past the Custom House when Spider suddenly pulled the car into the side of the road and cut the engine by pulling the wires apart. The windscreen wipers stopped in the middle of the glass and driven snow quickly began to coat the windscreen. He took a deep breath, calming himself before he turned to look at the young woman, sunk deep into the seat, only the tip of her nose showing over her raised collar.

'What's wrong?' he asked.

Judith shook her head.

'Talk to me. What's wrong?'

Judith shrugged, embarrassed now by her earlier outburst. 'You shouldn't have stolen the car,' she said eventually.

'We needed the car,' he said quietly. 'We wouldn't have been able to make it to the warehouse without one. And don't forget, we decided to follow Kathleen to see where they're storing the goods. How did you think we were going to follow them — on foot?'

'I don't know,' Judith finally admitted with a sigh. 'I just didn't think.'

Spider cranked down the window slightly, allowing a little of the chill air into the car, to help clear the misted-up windows. He thought he understood the curious mixture of emotions Judith was feeling; he had encountered similar reactions before from settled people ... he just never thought she'd have them. But then, he occasionally forgot that she was from that same settled, moneyed background. 'Judith, when you're living on the streets, you'll often end up doing things not because you want to, but because you have to. You'll steal food to survive: is that so wrong? You'll break into a building for shelter. You'll rob clothes to keep warm. You'll drink to forget and you'll take drugs to bring dreams that take you out of this world.' The pain in his voice was clear now, and she suddenly realised that he was close to tears. 'Because once you're in this world, Judith, there's no escape. Once you go on the streets, it's downhill all the way: crime, drugs ... worse.'

'It doesn't have to be that way,' she said fiercely.

'It does. Because there is no other way.' He reached in beneath the steering wheel again and wrapped the two wires together, starting the car.

~

The van slid into the alley behind the warehouse. It had taken nearly an hour and a half to travel out of the city centre. The snow showed no signs of letting up, and it was now freezing, coating the roads in a treacherous blanket.

Joe Ryan turned the key in the ignition and they sat in silence listening to the engine tick quietly to itself. Finally Kathleen swivelled around in her seat to look at her two brothers who were sitting in the back of the van, bundled up in heavy coats, thick gloves and scarves. They had balaclavas on their heads which they would pull down when they got into the warehouse. 'Ready?' she asked.

They both nodded.

Kathleen pointed out into the night. 'I don't see the security guard's car, so it's possible he didn't make it here with the condition of the roads. Be careful,' she said, and just when they were beginning to think they might be concerned about them, she added, 'I don't want any mistakes.'

Jed and Mickser slipped out of the back door of the van, sinking into packed snow that came up to their ankles. They climbed on to the roof of the van, hauling themselves up by the roof rack. When they were both in position, Jed hammered twice on the roof, and their father slowly and carefully backed the van right up to the warehouse wall. Jed hammered once, telling him to stop. The top of the wall had been spiked with slivers of glass and strands of barbed wire, but the brothers had come prepared with thick postal sacks which they laid across the wire. Mickser then simply stepped from the roof of the van on to the wall, swaying slightly in the breeze. Jed passed him over the thick length of rope which had been securely tied to the roof rack. Dropping the rope to the ground, Mickser carefully climbed down. Moments later, his older brother joined him.

As they clumped across the yard, Mickser pointed to the perfect footprints they were leaving in the snow, but Jed shook his head. He nodded at the falling snow. 'In five minutes, you'll never even know they were there.'

~

Spider turned left just before the Point Depot into a narrow side street. High buildings on either side protected it from the worst of the snow, and only the occasional flake made it on to the cobbles.

'This is it?' Judith asked.

'At the bottom of the street, we turn right. We should be facing the warehouse then. I didn't want to drive past it though, just in case we were spotted.' He turned off the headlights and drove down the street on sidelights, finally pulling in to the side before the turning. He pulled the wires apart, killing the engine. 'I'm getting out for a look. Stay here,' he said.

Judith wasn't inclined to argue. Although they street they were in was relatively clear of snow, she could clearly see that a blizzard was raging beyond.

'When I'm gone, lock the doors,' Spider said, and slipped from the car. She watched him hurry to the end of the street and peer around the corner. He turned his head and raised his hand before disappearing. She hoped he wasn't going to be long.

Spider darted across the empty road to the warehouse. There was no sign of a van, and he wondered if the Ryans had decided to cancel on account of the weather, or if they'd already come and gone. With his head ducked into the driving snow, flakes stinging his eyes, icy water trickling down the back of his neck, he decided to make a quick circuit of the building, before heading back to the car.

The snow cut visibility down to a few yards, and Spider had actually walked past the entrance to the narrow alley before the sound of metal doors sliding open stopped him. He turned back the way he had come ... and discovered the narrow opening. A delivery bay. He heard voices now, a muttered curse. He recognised Mickser's voice. And there was a peculiar whining noise which he couldn't immediately identify.

Spider crept into the alley, trying to make out what was happening at the other end. A pair of double doors were open, and so was the back of the van. With his back to the wall, he inched closer. Two orange lights appeared and the whining noise grew louder. A small fork-lift truck appeared, carrying a pallet with an enormous cardboard box on it. He spotted the numeral 10 on the box and a picture of a television, and he guessed that there were ten television sets inside the large box. One of the Ryan brothers — Jed, he guessed — drove the fork-lift right up to the van and eased the box inside. Spider watched while four identical boxes were loaded into the van. The sixth box however was taller and narrower, and held a consignment of videos.

Spider began to back out of the alley. Fifty television sets and at least as many videos! If the police caught them with this lot, Kathleen and her brothers would go to jail for a long time.

~

Something had happened. She was convinced of it. He had been gone far too long. Maybe he'd fallen and hurt himself on the icy road. Slipping out of the car, Judith pulled her coat tighter around her shoulders and padded out of the side-street into the blizzard. 'Spider?' she called.

~

The voice shocked him motionless. Spider turned. He could just about make out the dark figure at the mouth of the alley.

He was racing towards it, hoping she wouldn't speak again ....

'Spider?'

The van lights flashed on, bathing the alleyway in white light, picking out the crouching man and the young woman standing in the mouth of the alley, a hand raised to shield her eyes from the glare.

'Run!' Spider shouted. Behind him doors slammed and the van started. He heard shouts, Kathleen's voice amongst them, and the whirring of wheels spinning on packed snow.

Judith saw Spider running towards her and the van bearing down on him. She turned and ran.

The van was almost on top of him before Spider threw himself to one side, the heel of his left boot clipping off the bumper, the force of the blow numbing his entire leg. It sent him spinning into a snow drift which cushioned his fall. He was up immediately, but the pain in his leg forced him to the ground again. He saw the van bearing down on Judith, saw her zig-zagging on the icy street, saw her crash to the ground. The van slewed to a stop, and the side doors slammed open. Jed and Mickser hopped out and grabbed Judith, hauling her unceremoniously into the back of the van. She managed to scream once before the door slammed shut, and the van took off down the street, wheels spinning.

Spider gritted his teeth and staggered for the VW. He wondered how he was going to drive with his numb left foot.

═══════════════════════════════════════

16

The phone was ringing.

Maxwell Meredith came slowly, sluggishly awake, grop-
ing for the phone beside his bed while blinking at the clock.
It was ten minutes to four. 'Yes,' he mumbled, sitting up in
bed, knuckling sleep out of his eyes.

The line crackled, then a muffled voice asked, 'Maxwell
Meredith?'

'Yes. Who is this?'

'I think you would know me as Spider, Mr Meredith.'

A surge of adrenalin brought Maxwell fully alert. Reaching
over, he shook Frankie awake, then leaned across so that she
could listen in to the call.

'What do you want?' Meredith demanded. 'Where's
Judith? What have you done to her?'

'I've done nothing to her, Mr Meredith. But she's in trouble
now. I need your help. She needs your help.'

'What has happened? Is she all right?'

'As far as I know, she's all right.'

'What do you mean as far as you know. Isn't she with you?'

The line crackled again. 'No, not any more. Look, will you help me?'

'The police...' Maxwell began.

'No police,' Spider said quickly. 'Not if you want to see Judith alive again.'

'Are you threatening me?' Maxwell demanded.

'I'm just telling you how it will be. I want her back as much as you do. Judith has been taken by some fairly nasty types. If they see the police, they could hurt her. I don't want that.'

Maxwell looked at Frankie, eyebrows raised in a silent question. What was he going to do?

'Will you help me?' Spider asked as the silence grew.

'Of course I'll help you. What do you want?'

'Meet me in Parnell Square, at the side of the Garden of Remembrance. I'm driving a battered red VW. Remember, no police, but if you could bring half a dozen strong lads with you, it would help,' he added and hung up.

Maxwell Meredith listened to the crackling line for a few moments, before pressing the receiver to restore the dial tone. He slowly dialled Barbara Harper's home number from memory. He hoped the private detective was at home.

~

Spider replaced the receiver and limped away from the phone box. Although it had stopped snowing, the ground was lost beneath a white blanket that hid icy patches and concealed broken kerbs and dips in the footpath. The car was less than two hundred yards away but it took him nearly fifteen minutes to reach it. He was bathed in an icy sweat by the time he pulled open the door and collapsed inside. He opened his coat and pulled out the wheel brace he'd used to break into the phone box for the money to make the call to Meredith. If he'd been caught with the iron bar as he walked down the street, he would have been picked up for carrying a deadly weapon, and what would have happened to Judith then? Luckily, there were no police on patrol. Indeed, his was the only car parked on the square. Locking the doors, he lay down on the seat, his arms wrapped tightly around his chest. He wondered how long it would take Maxwell to reach him. He still wasn't sure that phoning Maxwell had been the best idea, but it was all he could think of. He hoped he could trust him not to bring any police.

When he'd finally managed to stagger back to the VW in the side-street opposite the warehouse, Spider found that his fingers were so numb he couldn't find the wires to start the car, and when he eventually got it going, he discovered that he couldn't put any pressure on his left leg; it kept slipping off the pedal. Gritting his teeth, he physically forced his foot on to the clutch and then slammed the car into gear and started out in the direction the van had gone. For a while he had been able to follow the fresh tracks on the snow-covered road, but further up the quays, close to the Financial Centre, they faded out and he'd been forced to accept that he had lost Judith. He had no idea where the Ryans had taken her.

The young man had sat in the car on the quays and felt the tears welling up in his dark eyes. What was he going to do? He couldn't go to the police: even if they did believe him — which was highly unlikely — what could they do? Nor would the travellers know where the Ryans were hiding.

But Tyrrell might.

The idea had stopped him cold. If anyone knew where the Ryans were bringing Judith, then Tyrrell would. And Tyrrell might be convinced to sell the information. There was no honour amongst thieves — just business.

But where was he going to get the sort of money Tyrrell would be looking for ...?

The answer was simple: Maxwell Meredith.

Slamming the car into gear, Spider set out to look for a phone box. He didn't want to think too closely about the decision; right now he was thinking about Judith.

When he'd made the call, he felt relief wash over him. The decision was made, and events were out of his control. As he'd been walking up from the phonebox, a ghost of a plan had slipped into place. But for it to have any chance of success, he'd need Maxwell Meredith's co-operation.

Closing his eyes, Spider attempted to sleep. His last thoughts were of Judith; he prayed she was safe.

~

Judith was going to vomit. Her head ached, she was bruised all over from the fall and from the long journey bouncing around in the back of the van. A dirty rag had been tied over her eyes and she had been gagged with a thin strip of rough cloth which split her lips at the corners of her mouth. The back of her throat was raw and her tongue felt swollen. She swallowed hard, knowing that if she threw up with the gag in her mouth, she could choke on her own vomit. Tears of frustration seeped out from beneath her blindfold. This was all her fault; if she'd remained in the car none of this would have happened.

Breathing deeply through her nose, Judith attempted to remain calm. But she was frightened, frightened for herself and terrified for Spider. In the instant before she'd fallen she'd seen him lying on the ground as if he'd been hit by the van. She hadn't seen him move. He could be lying in the gutter dead or dying, and it was all her fault. She tried to pray, but found that she couldn't remember any of her childhood prayers.

The van lurched to a stop. She heard sliding doors opening, icy air blasting into the van, and then rough hands grabbed her, hauling her out into the snow. Gloved hands caught her chin, squeezing her cheeks painfully. Even before she heard the voice, Judith knew it was Kathleen. 'I knew we'd meet again. And this time your boyfriend isn't here to protect you.'

~

Glass exploded all over Spider. As he struggled awake, rough hands grabbed his arms, his head, his hair and hauled him out of the car on to the road. He struggled, his street-fighting reflexes taking over, lashing out with hands and feet, feeling the blows connect, heard someone grunt in pain, a whispered curse. Then he was struck from behind, a sharp blow into the kidneys that jerked him upright in agony. Another blow sank into the pit of the stomach and he went down gasping for breath. He was picked up and slammed back against the car. He tasted blood in his mouth where he bit his tongue. Spider blinked away the spots of flashing light before his eyes and attempted to concentrate on his attackers. They were four burly men. He recognised their type immediately: bouncers or bodyguards.

A figure loomed up behind them, stepping into the pool of yellow light cast by the streetlight. Although he'd never seen Maxwell Meredith before, the resemblance to Judith was striking. Spider tensed, preparing for another beating.

'Let him go,' Maxwell Meredith commanded sharply, his voice ringing out in the bitterly cold air. The four men stepped away from the young man, though their eyes never left him. 'I told you I wanted him taken out of the car, not beaten to a pulp,' Meredith snapped.

Barbara Harper appeared from the opposite side of the VW and lifted the wheel brace she'd spotted on the floor of the car before her men had smashed in the windows. 'He was armed,' she said simply. 'We didn't want any accidents.' She moved away from the VW and returned to her own car, followed by the four men.

Maxwell Meredith and Spider faced each other in silence. They were both surprised by what they saw: Meredith was far tougher-looking than Spider had expected, his thin lips and cold unblinking eyes giving his face a cruel and ruthless aspect. Meredith's impressions of Spider O'Brien had been culled from the police reports; he expected to find himself looking at a vicious lout. But the young man facing him was darkly handsome and obviously intelligent, his eyes black against his pale flesh. Meredith knew that it must have taken extraordinary courage to have made the call to him, but only the rigid muscles in the young man's jaw revealed the tension he was under. Meredith admired the way he had coolly fought back against his attackers, and yet was now capable of facing the man who had brought the thugs. He stepped closer to the young man. 'My wife tells me that you're Judith's friend.'

'I am.'

The older man leaned forward. 'Why did you take her away?'

'I didn't,' Spider said simply. 'She insisted on coming with me. I couldn't stop her.' He shrugged. 'You know what she's like what she gets something into her mind. She's stubborn.'

'She gets that from me,' Maxwell said. He stretched out his hand. 'I'm Maxwell Meredith.'

Spider looked at it for a moment then grasped the man's hand and shook it. 'Spider O'Brien.'

'I didn't get a chance to thank you for looking after my daughter last summer,' Maxwell said. 'Frankie told me you kept Judith safe.'

'I tried to. I didn't always succeed though. I haven't kept her safe this time.'

Maxwell nodded towards his own car. 'Let's sit. We can talk.'

Maxwell opened the door of the Mercedes for Spider. The young man blinked in the warm atmosphere that smelt of leather and spice. He sank into the soft seat. Maxwell opened the driver's door and slid behind the wheel. He reached on to the back seat and lifted a thick-bodied flask. 'Frankie thought I might need this,' he said, unscrewing the cap and balancing it on his knees. The rich odour of freshly-brewed coffee filled the car. 'However, I think you might need it more than I do.'

Spider accepted the cup gratefully, wrapping both hands around it, bringing it close to his face, breathing in great lungfuls of the rich aroma. He sipped the coffee carefully, wincing as it stung his bloody tongue, but feeling the immediate effects of the caffeine. He finished the drink in two long swallows and then took his time drinking the second cup which Maxwell poured for him.

'I wasn't sure if you'd come,' Spider said eventually.

'I wasn't going to,' Maxwell admitted. 'I was going to phone the police and give them your location. Then I realised that might not be in Judith's best interests. The police are convinced you kidnapped her, you see. Apparently she phoned the station, saying that you were prowling around the grounds ....'

Spider nodded. 'Kathleen made the call.' He saw Meredith's blank expression and quickly outlined the events of the last three days, beginning with his first encounter with Judith on Saturday.

Maxwell listened in silence, only asking the occasional question when he wanted more information. He shook his head when he heard how Spider had nearly been run over by the van, and his expression hardened when he learned that Judith had been grabbed off the street.

'Do you know where they've taken her?'

Spider shook his head. 'I don't, but the man Tyrrell I mentioned earlier, he might know. That's why I phoned you. I need your help to ask him.'

'Will he tell us?'

Spider's grin was savage. 'He'd sell his own mother for profit. So he can either sell us the information, or we can have those four lads ask him. But I'm not leaving without finding Judith's whereabouts,' he said grimly.

Meredith glanced quickly at Spider, surprised by the emotion in his voice. 'Do you love her?' he asked quietly.

Spider returned his look. 'I don't know. Once I would have said yes, but now I'm not so sure anymore. I like her a lot though,' he added. Then he asked, 'Was that the answer you were looking for?'

Meredith nodded. 'You travelled together for a week and now you've been together for two days. You barely know each other. It was the right answer.'

~

'What are we going to do with her?'

Judith was beginning to recognise the different voices. There were two young men, an older man and Kathleen. She thought it was Mickser who had spoken.

'I mean, she's no use to us, is she?'

'She owes us,' Kathleen said quietly.

'Spider owes us,' Jed said.

'The girl caused all the trouble,' Kathleen said.

Their voices echoed slightly and Judith guessed that they were in a large room or a garage. It was bitterly cold and she was sitting on a damp concrete floor. Water dripped in the distance.

There was a cough and then the older man said, 'She's wealthy. Seems a shame to waste an opportunity like that.'

There was a long silence, and then Kathleen said quietly. 'She's very wealthy. Her Da's one of the richest men in Ireland. He'd pay a pretty penny to have his little girl back, wouldn't he?'

'I'm having nothing to do with this!' Mickser said defiantly. 'This is kidnapping.'

'Nor I,' Jed muttered.

'You'll do as you're told,' Kathleen snapped. 'This is a chance to make some big money. Real money. I wonder how much Daddy would pay for his little girl?' she continued, thinking aloud.

'What about Spider?' Jed asked.

'What about him?' Kathleen sneered. 'He's running scared. We won't see him again in a hurry.'

~

'It's the guy who was here earlier,' Tommy shook Tyrrell awake. 'The guy who nearly broke my arm. He wants to sell something.'

Tyrrell sat up in the bed and looked at Tommy unbelievingly. 'You wake me a five-thirty just to tell me that someone wants to sell me something. Tell him to come back later.'

'Says he can't. Says he's too hot; so are the goods.'

Tyrrell swung his legs out of bed, peach-coloured silk pyjamas rustling. 'This better be worth it,' he muttered, 'else you're going to be looking for another job.'

Tyrrell stamped into the sittingroom to find Spider sitting in his leather swivel chair. 'This better be worth it, Spider,' he snarled. 'You turn up out of the blue, assault one of my staff and generally make my life difficult. And now you're back at half-five with something that can't wait. What is it?'

'Turn off the light,' Spider said quietly.

Tyrrell looked at him for a moment, then slapped the wall, knocking off the lights.

Spider crossed to the window and opened the venetian blinds. Parked outside the door was a sleek snow-spattered black Mercedes.

'I don't deal in cars, Spider, you know that,' Tyrrell said.

'This is the luxury model,' the young man said slowly, ignoring him, 'leather seats, power-steering, electric everything, a CD player in the car instead of cassettes.'

Tyrrell looked at the car again; it was a beauty. The sort of car he always dreamed of owning himself. 'How hot is it?'

'The owner doesn't even know it's missing yet.'

'Why didn't you take it to Bob on the Strand or Paddy on the Naas Road. They deal in hot motors.'

'Thought I'd do you a favour,' Spider said, smiling easily. 'Figured I owed you one.'

'How much?' Tyrrell asked.

'Gimme a fair price, plus the necklace the girl gave you this morning.'

'Seven-fifty,' Tyrrell said immediately.

'A grand,' Spider countered. 'And the necklace.'

Tyrrell stuck out his hand. 'Deal.'

Five minutes later, Spider padded out to the Mercedes, the thousand pounds and Judith's necklace zipped up in his inside pocket. Tyrrell, bundled up in a heavy suede coat and fur-lined boots, followed, while the bodyguard waited by the door. He'd been instructed to make breakfast. Spider opened the passenger door and Tyrrell climbed in, rubbing the butter-soft leather and real wood dashboard. Even if he never drove it himself, he could sell it for twenty times what he'd paid Spider.

Spider climbed in and started the car. He revved it, the sound barely audible. 'Like it?' he asked.

Tyrrell nodded. 'You know, I'm proud of you, Spider. I always knew we could do business together.'

Spider put the car in gear and drove down through the snow to the bottom of the road. He turned left, then pulled in to the kerb and switched off the engine. When he turned to a puzzled Tyrrell, his face was grim. 'Now, I only have one question for you, and I'm not in the humour for any crap. Kathleen Ryan and her brothers have snatched the girl I was with this morning. I want to know where they've taken her.'

'Don't be ridiculous,' Tyrrell snapped. He attempted to get out of the car, but Spider caught him by the collar of his coat and hauled him back inside.

'Answer my question.'

'You're making a big mistake, boy. You can go to hell!'

The car door was abruptly wrenched open and Tyrrell hauled out into the bitterly cold morning air. He was pushed up against a stone wall by four large men.

Spider climbed out of the car and leaned on the snow-covered bonnet. 'Do you want to answer me ... or them?'

17

Maxwell Meredith drove as fast as he could on the icy road. Spider sat beside him, hands dug deep into his pockets, though he wasn't cold. Occasionally, he glanced around to make sure that the private detective was following in the Land Rover with her three men. One had been left behind to look after Tyrrell and his man, and to ensure that he didn't try to contact the Ryans.

Faced with the four men, Tyrrell had been delighted to tell them all he knew about the Ryans and their activities. He had also given them the address of a derelict house out beyond the airport, which the Ryans used to store their stolen goods until they could be safely disposed of.

The Mercedes was passing the church in Whitehall when the carphone chirped, jerking Spider awake. He looked around blankly before he realised what was making the noise. Gripping the wheel tightly, his eyes still firmly fixed on the road, Maxwell Meredith instinctively reached for the receiver, 'Yes?' he said. He listened for a few moments, then immediately indicated and pulled in to the side of the road. The heavy car slid as he pressed too hard on the brakes.

'When did this come in? What exactly did they say?'

The Land Rover pulled in behind the Mercedes and Barbara Harper jumped out. When she saw that Meredith was on the phone, she pulled open the back door and climbed in.

'No! No police. When they phone again, agree to everything,' Maxwell said and hung up. He sat in silence for a moment, then turned in his seat so that he could look at both Spider and Harper. 'Frankie's just got a call from someone claiming to be Spider O'Brien,' he said calmly. 'He is looking for a ransom of one million pounds in return for Judith's safe return. If we don't have an answer in the next hour, he is threatening to cut off one of her fingers and send it as proof of his intentions.'

Spider clenched his fists so tightly that his nails dug into the flesh of his palm. 'Kathleen,' he whispered.

'Will they do it?' Maxwell asked quietly.

Spider took a deep breath before he nodded. 'She could. She has a vicious streak in her.'

Barbara Harper leaned in across the front seat. 'How far to this address?'

Spider shrugged. 'Normally ten minutes. But in this weather it could be half an hour ... and that's only if we find the place immediately.'

'We'd better hurry,' the detective said and slipped out of the car.

Spider and Meredith looked at each other, recognising the pain mirrored in their eyes. Without a word, Meredith pulled the car on to the empty road, packed snow spinning from beneath his wheels.

~

'Do you think you're worth a million pounds,' Kathleen Ryan knelt in front of Judith and looked deep into her eyes. The fact that they had removed her blindfold and gag frightened Judith even more than being held prisoner. She'd read somewhere that kidnappers only did that when they weren't going to free their prisoners. They were no longer worried about being recognised ... because there would be no-one around to recognise them!

Judith had forgotten how big Kathleen was. She was tall and broad, her features square and almost masculine, though the skin on her face was slightly puffy, and there were deep black rings beneath her brilliant green eyes. Her thick mane of fiery red hair had been parted in the middle of her head, then tied back into a long ponytail.

Kathleen slapped her hard, the sudden blow cracking her head to one side. 'I asked you a question,' she snarled.

Judith felt as if her whole face was on fire. No-one — no-one — had ever struck her before. 'I'm worth a million,' she muttered, blinking furiously, but determined not to cry in front of Kathleen. She could feel her lip begin to swell.

Kathleen nodded. 'I hope so.' She reached into her coat and took out a black-handled clasp knife. With a long dirty nail, she pulled it open. The curved blade locked with a snick. 'You see, I told them that if they didn't give me an answer, I was going to cut off one of your fingers ... just to prove how serious I am.'

Judith stared in disbelief at the young woman, but saw nothing but hate in her eyes.

Kathleen folded the knife away. She stood up. 'And you might be interested to know that the call came from your boyfriend.'

Judith watched the girl clump away. She paused at the door that led into another room and snapped off the lights. The three flickering buzzing flourescents died with a crackle, plunging the room into darkness. Judith relaxed against the heavy wooden work bench she'd been tied to. Kathleen terrified her; she had never seen such raw emotion in anyone's face before. The girl would cut her with the blade without a second thought. Not so long ago Judith had actually hated her stepmother, but she didn't think she had ever hated her with such a passion.

Judith attempted to move her legs, wincing with the effort, biting back a retort. She was sitting on the icy concrete floor, her legs stretched straight out in front of her. Her bottom was numb and there was a solid pad of pain at the small of her back.

In the dim light it was difficult to make out any details of her surroundings, but Judith thought she was in a garage or long shed. The high room was filled with numerous cardboard boxes, and the haul of televisions and videos had been piled up along the wall. A large gilt mirror with a crack running through it was resting up against the opposite wall, while a dozen chairs, a mixture of styles and periods, were piled beside it. Half-glimpsed under tarpaulins were tables, chairs, lamps and sideboards as well as television sets, radios, stereos and computers: the remnants of the Ryans' burglaries.

She tested her bonds. Her wrists had been tied behind the legs of the bench with thick cord which bit into the soft flesh of her wrists. She tried rubbing the cord against the leg of the bench, but she only succeeded in chafing the skin off her wrists. She felt something hot coil down into the palm of her hand and realised with horror that her wrists were bleeding. Tears of frustration and pain squeezed out from beneath her tightly closed eyes. She jerked against the table in a fit of temper ... and heard something hard and metallic roll off the table and clatter on to the floor to her right. She held her breath, expecting Kathleen, whom she feared more than any of the others, to come back into the room. When no-one appeared, she squirmed around on the floor, digging in her heels to manoeuvre herself around. The pain at the base of her spine became agonising and she felt as if her shoulders were being pulled from their sockets. Her heel touched something. It rolled away from her. Gritting her teeth, Judith extended her left foot and stretched as far as she could, trying to reach beyond the object so that she could drag it back.

There were voices in the hallway outside.

Judith scrambled to get back into position. She was bathed in sweat which quickly chilled on her body. Her arms and legs were throbbing and her wrists felt as if they were on fire.

The light snapped on and Mickser stepped into the garage. He hurried across to Judith and crouched down beside her. He had a mug of tea in his hand. 'Here, drink this,' he said quickly, 'before Kathleen notices I've gone.' Holding the back of Judith's head, he brought the chipped mug to her lips. She sipped carefully, feeling the hot oversweet liquid scald her tongue, then burn its way down into her stomach.

'Thank you,' she whispered. As she dipped her head to drink again, she glanced sideways to where the object had fallen from the table. It was a chisel. And all Mickser had to do was look around and he would see it! She drank again, then looked up at the young red-haired man, looking into his green eyes. 'Why does Kathleen hate me?' she whispered.

He dropped his gaze and shook his head. 'Drink,' he insisted, pressing the cup against her lips.

'I've done nothing to her,' Judith persisted.

Mickser sighed. He snatched a quick glance over his shoulder at the door. 'Kitty thinks she would have been married to Spider by now if you hadn't come along. She hasn't really been lucky with boys. She had a boyfriend before, but he went off with another girl. Then she latched on to Spider, thought she'd have him ... told everyone they were going to be wed, though I told her he wasn't the marrying kind. Then you came along. Now she blames you because she thinks she's been shamed again. Drink!' he commanded before Judith could ask another question. He stood up and crossed to the door. 'Don't tell her I've been here,' he said as he snapped off the light.

The sweet tea had revived her, given her a sudden burst of energy. And at least she now knew what she was reaching for; it would have been terrible to make all the effort and find she'd snared something useless. Now that she had the location of the chisel fixed in her mind's eye, it was easier to stretch out her foot and catch it. Slowly, wincing every time the metal tip scraped off the stone floor, she pulled in her leg, dragging the chisel closer. Then, drawing her legs up beneath her, until she was squatting, she managed to drag the chisel with the sole of her shoe up beneath her thigh. By squirming around the leg of the bench, she managed to touch it with her fingertips.

Suddenly, there was a light in the hallway outside and voices echoed off the walls.

Judith jerked herself savagely against the leg of the table, actually inching the whole thing forward ... just enough for her to catch the cold metal between first and second fingers. Pulling the chisel behind her back, she squirmed around and stretched out her legs. Although her breath was coming in great heaving gasps, and she was soaked with the effort, she forced herself to breath normally. Behind her back, her hands were busy, manoeuvring the chisel blade against the thick ropes, sawing it up and down, feeling the thick cord give a little. She gasped in sudden pain as the razor sharp edge sliced through skin.

The voices outside the door were arguing. Kathleen's strident voice was clearly audible. 'The hour is up. I'm going to get Jed to phone again. If they give us any run-around, we'll send them a finger.'

Another voice — the older man she thought — murmured something, and Kathleen snapped. 'How much more trouble can we get ourselves into? And we're only in trouble if the police catch us. But they won't. Think of it, Da ... a million pounds. It'd be like winning the lottery. We could go away, do anything we wanted. It's a once-in-a-lifetime opportunity.'

The older man spoke again, but Judith didn't hear what he was saying. Her heart was thundering, blood pounding in her ears.

'It's seven now,' Kathleen said. 'Get Jed to make the call. Remind him to say he's Spider. If they agree to our terms, we'll phone them back with the arrangements.'

Footsteps vanished down the hall and Judith was just beginning to relax when the light snapped on and Kathleen stepped into the room. She came and stood over Judith with her hands on her hips, before crouching down in front of her.

'We're going to phone home to see if your Da will play ball. For your sake, he'd better.'

'And if he doesn't?' Judith wondered. She was desperately trying to hold on to the chisel, but it was slick with blood and sweat. She felt another strand of the thick cord give way.

Kathleen grinned, showing discoloured teeth. 'I'll bet a nice girl like you plays piano,' she said quietly.

Surprised, Judith nodded.

'Well, if your Da doesn't co-operate, you'll be playing with one hand from now on.'

Judith asked the same question she had put to Mickser. 'Why do you hate me?'

'Because you took Spider from me.'

'He was never yours in the first place ....'

Kathleen put her face right up against Judith's. Her breath was hot and foul. 'He would have been!' she shouted. 'Until you came along, with your fancy clothes and posh accent. And you took him! He wasn't your kind; you'd no right to do that.'

'He wasn't your kind either.'

'He's a traveller, like me!'

'He's a traveller,' Judith said proudly, 'but you're no traveller. You're nothing but a thief.'

Kathleen showed her teeth again. 'And do you think your precious boyfriend's never stolen?'

'I'm sure he's stolen to survive. But that's not what you're doing. He's not a thief,' Judith said defiantly. Suddenly her hands were free. Gripping the chisel tightly, she forced herself to sit still and wait, biding her time.

'There's more to Spider than you'll ever know, girl. He should have wed me. Maybe if we had been wed, I wouldn't be doing this.'

'I suppose that's my fault too,' Judith snapped. 'Everyone's fault but your own. Why can't you accept that Spider wanted nothing to do with you. He saw you for what you were.'

Suddenly the knife was in Kathleen's hand, the metal cold against Judith's cheek. 'You've got a smart mouth on you.'

'Kathleen!' Jed's voice broke the spell as he strode into the room. 'They've agreed to everything. One million pounds in small unmarked bills. They'll have it ready at noon.'

'It's a trick,' Kathleen said immediately, straightening up. 'They've given in too easily. Tell me exactly what he said.'

'I spoke to the woman again,' Jed said. 'I told them I was Spider, asked them did they agree. She said yes, they'd have the money at twelve, and I hung up.'

Kathleen frowned. 'Where's her father? He should have been there. They're up to something. Get back on to the phone. Insist that you speak to him.'

'Why?'

'I don't know. Just do it.'

As her brother hurried away, Kathleen turned back to Judith, the knife glittering wickedly as she folded it away. 'I hope, for your sake, that they're not being stupid.'

18

'Are you sure this is the place?' Maxwell Meredith asked Spider. They were crouched behind a line of tall snow-capped bushes looking at a dilapidated two-storey house set in its own grounds. At one stage fire had eaten through it, the black scorch marks still clearly visible against the brickwork and above the boarded-up windows. Even though snow covered most of its wounds, they could see where a portion of the roof was missing.

'This is the place.' Spider pointed to tyre tracks in the snow that led towards the large double garage that adjoined the derelict house.

Maxwell squirmed around to look at Barbara Harper who was standing behind him. 'Well — what do you suggest?'

'Call the police,' she said simply.

'No police,' Spider said immediately, and Maxwell nodded. 'No police.'

One of Harper's men scurried through the piled snow. 'Call for you sir, from your wife. She says they've phoned back and are demanding to speak to you this time.'

'They know something is wrong,' Spider said urgently. 'We have to move now.'

'What do you suggest?' Maxwell asked.

'I'll go forward and try to find out where they're keeping her. Once we get her out, then you can call the police.'

Barbara Harper shook her head. 'I cannot agree.'

'I'm not asking you to agree,' Spider hissed, 'and I'm not asking for your permission. I'm telling you what I'm going to do.'

'If the people in the house spot this young man,' Harper said urgently to Meredith, 'they could hurt your daughter.'

'If they see the police, they'll certainly hurt her,' Spider snapped. He pushed his way through a gap in the bushes and ran limping across the overgrown lawn, now treacherous because the snow hid the potholes and other obstacles. He knew there was little danger of being seen. If the Ryans were in the house — and he prayed they were — then they would be at the back where lights wouldn't be seen from the road. He fell once, his already tender ankle twisting on a hidden stone and tumbling him to the ground. He lay in the snow, breathing deeply as fire throbbed in his foot. He could feel it swelling and hoped he wouldn't have to cut his boot off. Gritting his teeth, he climbed to his feet and staggered on. Judith needed him. It has been a long time since anyone had needed him.

Spider crept around the side of the house, ducking beneath the windows, until he realised that they'd all been painted black from the inside. However, a wan strip of light was visible beneath the kitchen door, and he could hear muted voices. He recognised Joe Ryan's growl. A portion of the diningroom window was missing and had been replaced by a sack. He pressed at the sacking carefully, then pushed until he heard pins drop to the floor and the cloth came free. Hauling himself up, he dropped into the room, crouching on the bare floorboards, almost expecting the door to burst open. When nothing happened he rose to his feet and then, testing each step before he put his weight on it, he inched his way forward.

The voices were clearer now. He could recognise Jed and Mickser's. He wondered where Kathleen was.

~

Kathleen sat on a cardboard box watching Judith intently, memorising every detail of her face, wondering what Spider saw in her. Was it her blond hair, or maybe her flawless skin, her snow-white teeth or her puppy-dog eyes? Kathleen Ryan's hair was red and coarse, her skin was speckled with black-heads and she had a rash of pimples across her forehead, her teeth were yellow and uneven. Her eyes, cold and green, were her best feature, but they were ringed with lines, the pupils yellowed with broken veins.

'Did you sleep with him?' she asked suddenly.

Judith looked shocked. 'I did not!'

Kathleen nodded, not entirely convinced. 'Did he find you attractive?'

Judith shook her head. 'I don't know. He never said.'

'He used to find me attractive. He said so. Do you think I'm attractive?'

'Yes.'

'Liar!' Kathleen suddenly spat. 'I'm not blind. I know what I see when I look into a mirror. You've had hot water every day of your life; you've never known what it's like to be dirty. I bet you wash your hair every day, don't you?' she demanded.

Judith nodded.

'Takes me an hour to wash my hair,' Kathleen said quietly. 'I have to boil the kettle, then add cold water to get the temperature right. I wash my hair, use the shampoo, then wait until the kettle boils again before I can rinse. And then I do it all over again. If I wash my hair once a week, I'm lucky.'

Judith said nothing.

Kathleen slid off the box and squatted before Judith. 'You've got such clear skin. I bet you use creams and mois-turisers every night ... that fancy cream with herbs in it. I use soap when I can, but often there isn't any.' She reached out and touched Judith's cheek with her fingertips. Judith winced and attempted to draw back. 'It's so soft. I bet Spider liked touching your skin.' She sat back on her haunches and the black-handled knife appeared in her hand. She turned the knife so that the light from the blade reflected into Judith's eyes. 'Such soft skin,' she murmured. She patted her own cheek, rubbed the flat of her hand across her forehead, feeling its coarse, rough texture.

Judith knew, in the instant before she saw the look in the other woman's eyes, that Kathleen was going to cut her with the knife, scar her face. She saw her thin lips curl with the thought ....

Judith Meredith lashed out with the chisel, the point of the blade nicking Kathleen's chin, the shock knocking her off her haunches, sending her sprawling.

Judith surged to her feet, groaning aloud as her numb legs protested. She hobbled away from Kathleen who was screaming obscenities.

Joe Ryan ran into the room, drawn by his daughter's screams. He saw Judith coming at him with a blade and instinctively ducked away, and then Judith was out in the darkened hallway. She ran towards the light and straight into Mickser. He caught her arm, twisting it savagely, sending the chisel flying. 'She's going to kill me,' Judith whispered. 'You've got to help me please!' she begged. Mickser hesitated — and Judith kneed him in the groin, doubling him up. Judith turned and ran back into the hall. Mickser shouted, grabbing for her hair, coming away with a handful of blond strands.

He hobbled into the hall. The girl was struggling with the locks on the front door, but he knew they wouldn't work, they were rusted shut. His big hands closed into fists. He was going to make her pay for what she'd done to him. He saw her turn, saw her eyes widen with fear ... and something else, something like astonishment. He was turning to see what she was looking at when something hit him hard across the back of the head and the floor raced up to meet him.

'Spider,' Judith breathed. 'I knew you'd come.'

~

Maxwell Meredith thought his heart was going to stop when he heard the girl screaming. It was Judith, he was convinced of it. 'Call the police now!' he shouted at Barbara Harper and then, followed by the three bodyguards, raced for the house. Two of the men hit the front door at a run, ripping it from its hinges, sending it crashing into Mickser who was attempting to sit up. He collapsed without a sound.

Judith and Spider were sitting on the stairs when Maxwell came running up. Spider's arm was around the girl, and her head was resting on his shoulder. Maxwell leaned against the door frame, breathing hard, looking from Judith to Spider.

'Nice timing,' Spider nodded.

'The police are on their way,' Maxwell gasped.

Judith looked from her father to Spider in astonishment. Standing up, Spider pressed his forefinger to her lips, stopping the multitude of questions. He helped her down the stairs and into her father's arms.

The three bodyguards appeared, holding Jed and Joe Ryan. Only Kathleen was struggling. When she saw Judith and Spider she went into a paroxysm of struggling.

Maxwell looked at each of the Ryans in turn. Police sirens were clearly audible on the sharp morning air. 'If you'd stuck to robbery, you'd have ended up with four or five years. However, kidnapping is a very serious offence. I would imagine you'll get fifteen years apiece.'

Putting one arm around Judith and the other around Spider, he turned back across the snow-covered garden. 'Let's see if we can keep you out of jail, Spider,' he said quietly.

'Seán,' Spider said suddenly.

'I beg your pardon?'

'It's not Spider, it's Seán.'

'Seán,' Maxwell Meredith said, nodding.

Monday 22nd February

19

The parcel arrived in the post. Frankie was sorting through the mail, dividing it into business and personal when she came across the small box with Judith's name carefully inked on the brown paper. It had been posted in London, but there was no return address. Frankie weighed the box in her hands. She had a very good idea who had sent the parcel.

A month had passed since that terrible weekend. The Ryans were in custody awaiting trial, and only Maxwell's money and contacts had kept Spider from joining them in jail. Maxwell had offered Spider money, but the young man had refused, saying he was travelling to England to look for work. When Maxwell had offered to find him a job to allow him to settle down, Spider had thanked him politely and shaken his head. He wanted to do some travelling first before he settled down.

'Judith,' Frankie called, raising her head to look up the stairs. 'Parcel for you.'

~

It had taken an enormous effort of will to carry the parcel unopened back up to her room. But once inside, with the door firmly shut behind her, she tore off the paper ... and discovered a cigarette box. Inside the box was the gold necklace she had given to Tyrrell.

'I'll get it back for you,' Spider had promised. And he had. Spider always kept his promises.

There was no message, but a large black spider had been drawn in felt tipped marker on to the box.

Her fingers were very steady as she fixed the necklace around her neck. She knew he'd be back.